*For brothers'
devotion to each other . . .
related or not.*

The
Thundering
Underground

JAKE THOENE and LUKE THOENE

TYNDALE KIDS
TYNDALE HOUSE PUBLISHERS, INC., CAROL STREAM, ILLINOIS

BAKER STREET
DETECTIVES 4

The Thundering Underground

Visit Tyndale's exciting Web site for kids at cool2read.com

Also see the Web site for adults at tyndale.com

TYNDALE and Tyndale's quill logo are registered trademarks of Tyndale House Publishers, Inc.

The Thundering Underground

Designed by Jacqueline L. Noe

Edited by Ramona Cramer Tucker

#JFIC 12-15-06
jmyst

Published in 1998 by Thomas Nelson, Inc., under ISBN 0-7852-7081-7.

First printing by Tyndale House Publishers, Inc., in 2006.

Library of Congress Cataloging-in-Publication Data

Thoene, Jake.
  The thundering underground / Jake Thoene and Luke Thoene.
    p. cm. — (The Baker Street detectives ; bk. 4)
    Summary: When Peachy has a run-in with the nephew of the tunnel construction foreman, the Baker Street Brigade discovers that the nephew may be the errand boy for an unsavory conspiracy.
  ISBN-13: 978-1-4143-0369-7 (hc : alk. paper)
  ISBN-10: 1-4143-0369-6 (hc : alk. paper)
    1. London (England)—History—1800-1950—Juvenile fiction.   2. Great Britain—History—Victoria, 1837-1901—Juvenile fiction. [1. London (England)—History—1800-1950—Fiction.   2. Great Britain.—History—Victoria, 1837-1901—Fiction.   3. Mystery and detective stories.] I. Thoene, Luke. II. Title. III. Series: Thoene, Jake. Baker Street detectives ; bk. 4.
  PZ7.T35655Th 2006
  [Fic]—dc22   2006007814

PROLOGUE

It was only four o'clock in the afternoon, but already the cold and dreary gray January sky drove the shopkeepers to shut their doors. It sent the homeless to their packing-crate hovels in alleyways and forced the rest of Londoners to retreat to their coal-stoked fires. Office workers hurrying north from the City, the financial district, wrapped their necks in scarves up over their ears.

The normal flow of pedestrians and horse-drawn carriages could not follow their usual routes home. A huge, plank-fenced yard occupied the center of Tottenham Court Road for more than three blocks. Posted every ten yards were signs: *Central and South London Rail—Keep Out!*

Behind twelve-foot-high gates scurried more than two hundred workmen. Some shouldered shovels and picks, while others drove mule teams hitched to cartloads of dirt.

In the center of the enclosure was a circus-ring-sized hole in the earth. A ramp sloped downward from view, quickly dropping beyond the reach of the dim light. Near the edge of the gaping chasm stood a shack that housed the offices of the foreman and the construction company owner.

An occasional low rumbling shook the ground, vibrating the shoe soles of the passersby and rattling the windows of the Oxford Street shops. Echoes resounded from the hole like the deep, breathy belches of an underground giant.

The City and South London Railway was not the first subterranean transport to be built in London. That distinction belonged to the Metropolitan Line, which had opened twenty-five years earlier, in 1863, and was an instant success. As London grew, more underground railroads were built, and still the public clamored for more lines to move more people faster. The City and South line, when finished, would link popular suburbs with the heart of commercial and financial London.

At a speed no greater than a snail's crawl, two men wheeled a covered cart down the sloping path. Another man in back gripped the brake handle tightly, keeping a continuous resistance on the wheels. The pair of men in the front joked ceaselessly.

"Hey, mate," one of them said to the other. "Have a care! If we lose this cart of dynamite it'll ruin the day of someone down below."

"Bumpsidaisy!" The other grubby worker chuckled. "But then they wouldn't have no burial costs, would they, Foreman Kelly?"

The brakeman, a burly man nicknamed Iron Kelly, snapped, "Real funny, Riley. If you don't straighten up, *I'll* bury you!"

They reached the bottom.

Kelly clicked his tongue twice. "Look sharp now. That's Mr. Ruby over there." He nodded toward a brawny man with a deeply wrinkled forehead, sun-bronzed skin, and bushy eyebrows. Charles Ruby was the owner of the construction company.

The foreman, Kelly, together with his helpers Riley and Chas, moved into the northbound tunnel. Over their heads, a million tons of dirt were supported by arching steel panels that ran along the completed segment of the tunnel, forming its tubelike shape. The three men stopped near a set of tracks, on which rested an empty handcar.

"Right," Kelly said, clamping the brake of the dynamite wagon.

"Swap it over." He motioned toward the rusty, hand-operated rail-car, then pulled back the tarp.

Riley and Chas did as he told them. Crate after crate of explosives was transferred. Then Riley and Chas pumped the handle of the car like children playing on a teeter-totter. Iron Kelly walked alongside carrying a lantern until they reached the head of the tunnel—a twenty-foot-high wall of solid rock. The wall was covered from floor to ceiling with two-inch-wide holes, spaced about eighteen inches apart. The holes had taken three days to drill. The pattern made the wall resemble a hive for gigantic, fearsome bees.

A stick of dynamite went in every hole, and attached to every stick was a fast fuse. There were about 250 explosive charges in all. All of the fuses were then tied together into a bundle that connected to one long detonation cord. "Can't think why we need so many," Chas complained. "Blow up half the town."

When it was completely prepared, Chas and Riley stood back while Kelly checked all the connections. Iron Kelly wiped the sweat from his head. "Right, you blokes. Let's get out of here." He pointed toward the handcar. "Chas, you and Riley clean up all these tools, load them, and get out. I'll go evacuate the rest of the tunnel. Give me ten minutes before you light the fuse."

"Sure thing, boss." Chas winked.

"You got eight minutes of fast fuse once it's lit, so edge! Cut along sharp, or you'll be strummin' a harp." Both helpers laughed at the old rhyme. It was a sort of good-luck charm among men handling explosives.

"Consider it done, Iron Kelly," Riley answered.

"Good," Kelly said, and he hurried off down the dark tunnel. The men watched as the light from his lantern grew dim and distant. Eventually the light disappeared entirely as Kelly went around a curve in the line.

Riley bit off the end of a cigar, then spit it out. The plug of tobacco bounced over the tangled mass of fuse. He scratched a match on his single remaining front tooth and began to puff.

"Have you gone dodgy?" Chas asked. "You'll blow us up!"

Riley shrugged. "I'm havin' me a cigar before I pick up any o' that garbage, see? Then I'll use it to light me fuse."

"You got no sense, Riley." Chas carried a heavy drill bit to the cart. He loaded several more tools while Riley just watched.

Finally Riley stooped and picked up a sledgehammer. A pile of hot ash from his cigar dripped to the ground beside the blasting cord. "That's enough," he said, tossing the hammer into the bucket and climbing up on the cart. "It's been about ten minutes, don't you think, Chas?"

"This business gives me the creeps," Chas remarked. "Light the thing so we can get out of here."

"You late for tea? If I'd have known you were in a hurry, I'd have lit it a long time ago." With that, Riley turned to face the coil of fuse and flicked his cigar. It struck the ground with a shower of sparks and rolled to a stop right next to the main fuse. The cord flared up brightly and began to burn with a noise like sizzling grease.

"Come on, Riley," Chas urged. "Edge!"

A few strong pumps on the handle and the handcar picked up speed.

Riley took his hands off the lever to rest them for just a second . . . and knocked the sledgehammer over the side. It bounded down across the tracks in front of the cart, causing the front wheels to derail and bounce on the wooden ties. The handle splintered.

As the axle ground on the rail, the two men fought to hang on. The car screeched to a halt.

"Now you've done it, you fool!" Chas yelled.

"Relax! It won't take long to fix."

Both men jumped down to put the cart back on the track. But it was heavier than it looked. Chas and Riley struggled to pick up the front end more than a couple inches off the ground.

"Now what are we going to do?" Chas shouted.

"We'll take out the tools so we can raise the front end," Riley replied, throwing the rest of the equipment off.

Chas stared back toward the head of the tunnel. He could see the tiny flicker as the fuse burned shorter.

"Don't stand there gawkin'!" Riley yelled. "Hurry up!"

Chas tossed the rock drill aside. Both men strained to lift the car. Riley's face turned a bright red. With one last grunt they raised the wheels over the track, dropping it into place. Chas climbed back aboard and began to pump the handle.

"Load the stuff again," Riley ordered.

"No time," Chas cried, pumping harder.

"You can't leave it. Ruby'll fire us if any of this stuff gets wrecked."

"I don't care! I want to get out of here with my life."

Riley stood in front of the cart, trying to hold him back, but the gearing in the operating system was so low that he did not stand a chance. His boots began to slip, and he was shoved backward. Just as he tried to jump aboard, his foot slipped, and the handcar knocked him out of the way. "Wait, Chas!" Riley screamed. "I'll be blown up!"

Chas did not wait or slow down, only pumped harder. The cart moved faster and faster. He looked back only once.

Why was Riley running the wrong way? Back toward the explosives?

Chas didn't pause long to wonder since the handcar was flying at full speed down the tunnel.

He heard a metallic clank, then another, as if the bolts securing the left front wheel had failed. Had the handcar been damaged by the derailment? Chas hadn't had time to check.

Just then the car flipped up in the air, spilling him into the darkness. It landed right on top of Chas, pinning him beneath it!

"Help!" he cried out.

But he knew that Riley had disappeared. By now the tunnel was deserted.

No help was going to reach him in time.

A second later a tremendous wind gusted by him with blinding force. He marveled at the shock wave of the massive explosion. It ripped along the passage, flinging boulders like cannonballs and iron bars like javelins.

It was the last thing Chas ever marveled at.

One

The stained-glass windows of the Whitefield Tabernacle Methodist Church on Tottenham Court Road shook with each blast that resounded through the floor. Dark-haired Danny Wiggins sat in the third pew from the front and jumped each time the boards rattled.

Reverend Mitchell Henry was having a difficult time with his sermon, hardly able to compete with the loud noises coming from the underground railroad construction site. "'O God,'" Henry quoted from Psalms. "'The nations have come into your inheritance; your holy temple they have defiled; They have laid Jerusalem in heaps.'"

Another blast interrupted him, covering his words.

Danny's friends Peachy Carnehan and Clair Avery sat to the boy's right. They were flanked on the opposite end by Clair's father, Inspector Jonathan Avery of Scotland Yard. Everyone listened as best they could to Pastor Henry's message, but the noise was too great to catch it all.

Danny saw Peachy hang his carrot-topped head and stare at his dangling feet. Duff Bernard, their big, slightly older friend, sat in the front row watching Reverend Henry with intensity. It seemed to Danny that Duff could hear what was being said, though no one else could.

All at once the blasts stopped, only to be replaced by a low rumble that rose gradually and went on for several minutes. The windowpanes shook again, and the wooden cross on the wall behind the platform rocked and fell. It bounced once, rested upright briefly, then spun around and clattered to the floor. Finally, the vibration stopped.

Pastor Henry stormed behind the altar and picked up the cross, holding it reverently in his hands. He laid it carefully against a chair and returned to the pulpit. "Ladies and gentlemen," he raged, "I do not know if *Jerusalem* is in danger of becoming rubble at this time. However, if we do not take some sort of action soon, this church will! I'm afraid we shall have to conclude today's service early because of the difficulty I have talking over all the noise. Thursday next we shall host a protest meeting at seven o'clock. All are welcome to come and express their concerns about the digging, so if you have friends who want—" He stared out the window.

Danny saw what had caught the pastor's attention. Black smoke spiraled into the winter sky. Fire alarms clanged. Shouts resounded.

Soon everyone in the building was straining to see out the window as the fire brigade's wagon drove hurriedly by.

"Let us pray," Henry said.

•••

"Accidents plague overbudget tunnel!" Danny yelled in his loudest newspaper-hawking voice. "Sunday sees second setback in seven days!" Duff stood beside him near the long line of covered market stalls, holding a supply of papers.

Across the cobblestones of Covent Garden's open square, Peachy competed with them. "Protesters rally to stop construction!" Peachy belted louder than Danny had. He cracked a competitive smile at them. It was a friendly rivalry but often fought with intense pride.

"I'll bet you a trip to the Marquis of Anglesey for lunch that I can sell off the lot before you," Danny called, pitching the idea to Peachy.

Peachy looked around at the mostly vacant scene. At a quarter of two in the afternoon the space between the broad roof of St. Paul's Church, Covent Garden, and the vegetable vendors was empty of shoppers. Still, anything to get out of the cold would be worth the work, even if it meant yelling one's voice out. "How about whoever first sells four papers wins? Loser stays and sells for both?"

"You're on," Danny replied.

Peachy scanned both directions and nodded confidently. "Right," he called, stepping away from the stalls and hopping up on the stone block of a horse-mounting step. The boy held up high a copy of the *Daily Telegraph*. "Get your paaaapers here!"

Danny tilted his head back to open his throat for another go. "Sunday fire follows earlier death! Second tunnel collapse this week!"

Peachy began to chuckle as an idea struck him. Perhaps the way to move papers was to make the news seem even more personal. He cupped his hands around his mouth. "Save your shop from rattling, cracking, and collapsing! Join the move to stop the digging!"

Just as he announced that, two dozen people seemed to come out of nowhere, rounding the corner of King Street into the square. "I'll take one of those, lad," a tall man with bushy side whiskers said. The neatly dressed fellow pitched two pennies into a tin plate on the ground below the mounting block.

"Thank you kindly, sir," Peachy replied, tipping his checkered cloth cap.

An older woman dressed all in black approached Danny and requested two papers. Danny snickered and waved at Peachy, but in the middle of his celebration the woman discovered she had misplaced her coin purse. She walked away, muttering to herself and digging through her handbag. Halfway across the plaza she found the small leather pouch and pulled it out. Since she was now closer to Peachy than Danny, she bought two papers from him.

Needing to sell only one more paper, Peachy laughed aloud, then turned to continue his pitch. "Filthy underground disrupts business!"

This particular statement got the attention of a curly-haired boy who appeared to be a few years older than twelve-year-old Peachy. The thin-faced newcomer with the sharp-pointed nose had just walked out of James Street, directly behind Peachy. He scowled at Peachy and walked toward him.

Peachy saw the angry look but never thought it was meant for him. He turned the other way to continue his pitch. "A protest today may save your shop tomorrow! Get the facts before it's too late."

"Hey!" The taller boy shoved Peachy from behind. "What do you mean yelling that kind of thing out?"

Peachy held his ground. "What's eating you, mate? I only sell the news, see?" He held up a copy to the angry-eyed boy.

"'Leave tunneling to moles,'" the boy read. He stared at it for a minute, then dropped the paper on the ground at Peachy's feet. "I'd find another line to read if I was you. Sure as my name is Billy Kelly, I know people that'd break your fingers for shouting that muck."

Peachy felt the hair on his neck stand up, the way it always did whenever this sort of confrontation happened. But the bully seemed not to notice.

Peachy caught Danny's eye, across the square. Danny nudged Duff and pointed. Peachy might need their help. Danny took a step toward his friend.

"So you don't like the news, then?" Peachy tried to make light of the incident. "Right, how about this one?" Peachy scanned the smaller stories for a substitute. "East Africa Company founded. One million pounds . . ."

"On second thought," the bully said, crossing his arms, "I think I *would* like one . . . gratis, see?"

"It's my last one." Peachy bent over to pick it up. "Seeing how it got soiled, take it."

Billy snatched it out of Peachy's hand and stalked off.

"Thanks for your business; come again," Peachy called out. But under his breath he mumbled, "And I'll drop a brick on your thick head."

By that time, Danny and Duff had made their way over to Peachy. "Was that bloke giving you a hard time, Peachy?" Duff asked in a gentle voice. Duff, though bulky in size, was soft-spoken and slow to get riled.

Peachy shook his head. "Naw, he just said he didn't have any friends, and when he asked me if I wanted to be one, I told him I don't even like dogs."

Duff giggled. "That's funny, Peachy! You thought he was a dog?"

Danny and Peachy both broke into laughter.

"Well, at least I'm done," Peachy asserted. "I win."

"Hold on there," Danny argued.

"No doubt about it," Peachy insisted. "The customer is always right."

Danny had opened his mouth to argue when Duff plucked his elbow. "I'm hungry," he complained. "Can Peachy go now and buy our lunch?"

Sighing, Danny gave in. "I'll get you next time." He dug into his jacket pocket. "Here's a shilling."

"Shall I make it three steaming-hot meat pies, then?" Peachy offered, closing his cold hand around the coin.

"Bring 'em back as fast as you can." Danny smiled.

"Yes, please," Duff agreed.

"Half a tick," Peachy assured them, and he darted off.

●●●

Peachy hurried along Great Russell Street, past the booth of the Punch and Judy puppet show. Punch hung forlornly out from the curtain, and Judy was nowhere in sight. There was no audience of young children on the wintry day. Out to Wellington Street he walked, where a left turn took him to the Marquis of Anglesey pub. Situated on a long triangular corner, the pub was easy to identify by its rounded brass doors, which matched the curve of the building.

It was always a treat to be the one to pick up lunch—to leave the work behind and stand, if only for a few minutes, in the warm pub. Peachy pulled the brass handle, and hot air rushed out to meet him. Once inside he pushed his way through the crowd of business-suited store clerks from the surrounding shops and overalled porters from the vegetable market.

"Three of those meat pies, please," Peachy said to the host.

"Sure thing, mate," the man agreed. "You plannin' on eatin' 'em all at once?" he joked. "Need a gallon o' cider to wash 'em down."

"Eat them?" Peachy acted surprised. "Why would I want to do that? I'm gonna put them in me pockets so's I can keep me 'ands warm," he replied, in imitation of the server's Cockney accent.

The man laughed. "'Ow are you, then, Peachy? Keeping well, I 'ope?"

"Just fine," Peachy agreed. "I kept out of a fight, sold all my papers, and won a bet, just so I can come down here for the grub."

"Very well, indeed. George," the host called, leaning halfway into the kitchen through the serving window. "Three meat pies, double-quick, for Master Peachy Carnehan. Pick out the biggest ones."

Despite all the cigar smoke floating about, Peachy half hoped that the food would take a long time to fix. His ears had grown hot and itchy the longer he waited, but he was feeling pleasantly warm and drowsy.

All too soon a pair of hands slipped a sack up on the pass-through. The host picked it up and, holding both of the top corners, spun the bag around itself. The bag wound up tightly, so the food would stay warm.

"Thanks," Peachy said, placing the coin on the counter and receiving his change.

"Always a pleasure," Peachy's friend answered. "See you next time."

Outside, the cold met Peachy like a brutal sock in the face. There was not even any snow, but the weather in London was so chilling it seemed as if it went straight to the bone.

Peachy retraced his steps down Wellington. At the corner of Russell he continued to the left, hoping that a different route back to Covent Garden would keep him longer out of the howling wind.

He was almost to Southampton Street on the outskirts of Covent Garden when he did a double take while passing an alleyway and spotted the kid who had tried to bully him earlier. Billy something, his name was. Peachy quickly jumped back out of sight and hid behind some wooden crates at the top of the alley.

Peering through the slats and around crates of discarded cabbage and rotting turnips, Peachy could see the boy standing outside a rusty metal door. The curly-haired youth looked impatiently around, as if he was waiting for something. Peachy ducked to avoid being seen.

A creak from seldom-used hinges echoed through the moist air, and Peachy heard a man's voice say, "Here now, don't lose these. They are extremely important plans."

"Don't worry," the tall boy remarked snidely. "It'd be my neck, too."

Peachy could see the front of the building from where he was hiding. *London Surveyors' Office,* the sign above the door said. Peachy wondered what was up that they would be meeting in an alley. Peeking again between slats and cabbages, Peachy saw a short, nervous-looking man.

"Tell him to give me better notice next time. And tell him it's going to cost him more," the man said.

"Sure," Billy replied. "Here," he continued, handing over a small roll of cash. "It's all there."

"I don't need to count it, then." The man nodded, took a step back, and shut the door. Billy turned away from Peachy and walked in the opposite direction, making a left turn at the end of the alley.

Instinctively Peachy jumped up to follow. Maybe it would turn out to be a mystery worth investigating. He had forgotten the Baker Street Brigade's lunches, even though he still clutched the bag.

Peachy ran down to the end of the alley, checking to see if it was clear for him to go farther. The curly-haired boy was already across the street and nearly to Chandos Place. As Peachy waited to see where he went next, Billy scooted into another alley and down toward Charing Cross Road.

Peachy knew exactly how to cut him off without taking the same route. But when Peachy arrived at the intersection of Charing Cross and St. Martin's Lane, Billy was nowhere in sight. Peachy worried that his quarry might have turned off a different way, but then he spotted him coming out of an alley.

Billy was casually carrying the rolled-up tube of paper under his right arm. The boy stopped at the edge of the busy street, waited for a four-horse team pulling a coal wagon to pass, then headed toward Peachy.

Peachy's heart sank. All he could do was pull his cap down across his eyes and face a shopwindow as if he were looking at something.

It worked. The boy passed right by Peachy without even a glance.

A moment later Peachy was on the other side of the street, following him about half a block behind.

At the next corner the road branched off in five directions. Billy took the second left, then a quick right. Peachy continued to follow, but in his haste to not lose his quarry, he was almost run over by a carriage. The team of horses reared and plunged, and the driver yelled at him. More concerned with the boy seeing him than being run over, Peachy ducked back behind the carriage.

"You mangy filth!" the driver shouted. "Why don't you watch out?"

Peachy stood on tiptoe to try to see over the crowd and through a double line of backed-up wagons and cabs. "Blast!" Peachy moaned. "Lost him already."

He raced out into the street, into the first gap in traffic he could find. Jogging down the lane where he had seen his target heading, Peachy came to the corner where Charing Cross Road joined Tottenham Court Road. Or rather, where Tottenham Court Road would have been if the street had not been barricaded with a wooden fence. Milling around outside the barrier were a couple hundred protesters and, it seemed, a million other people angry at the congestion and the turmoil. After the emptiness of Covent Garden, it now seemed that all of London was crushed into Tottenham Court Road.

Then he got an unexpected break. "Aha!" he exclaimed. Peachy spotted the tall boy entering a gate that led into the construction yard of the underground railroad.

Peachy fought his way through the mass of protesters and onto the grounds of the construction site. He was only ten yards behind the boy now.

Then he was grabbed by the back of the collar.

A security guard demanded, "Where do you think you're goin', mate? Waltzin' in so breezy an' all?"

"I'm with my friend there," Peachy scrambled to answer. "I was just—"

"You were just leavin', I think," the guard replied, dragging Peachy by the arm out to the street.

Peachy yanked his elbow away from the man and stumbled clumsily into the horde of chanting protesters. He was angry, frustrated, and now, he noticed, tired and hungry. Spotting a fire in a barrel where a sidewalk vendor roasted chestnuts, he moved closer.

"Right nice to warm yer hands on a cold day, ain't it?" the chestnut man said in a gruff voice. "Warm chestnuts treat yer innards the same way, miss."

Miss? Peachy had thought the chestnut seller was talking to him. *Guess not.* He peered closer to see the person the man addressed.

The girl was bundled up in a woolly coat and scarf. And she was cute, too, Peachy noticed. Then he realized . . . "Clair!" Peachy greeted Inspector Avery's daughter happily. "I'm surprised to see you here."

"And I thought you and Danny and Duff had to sell papers today." She smiled.

"We did, but I met this bully who was picking on me. And then I saw him again down this alley, and he looked like he was up to something dodgy, so I followed him. He went in there." Peachy pointed at the gates with the bag of meat pies. "Oh no!" he said, looking at the now-squashed bag. "They're gonna be so mad."

"What?" Clair asked.

"Danny and Duff," Peachy said, swatting his head with his free hand. "I was supposed to take them this lunch, but I completely forgot." He began to hustle back toward Covent Garden. "Clair," he called over his shoulder, "do you want to come with me?"

"To see the chums? Sure!" Clair hurried to catch up with him. "And I want to hear about this mysterious bully!"

"Come on, then." Peachy motioned with his head. "I'll tell you all about it on the way."

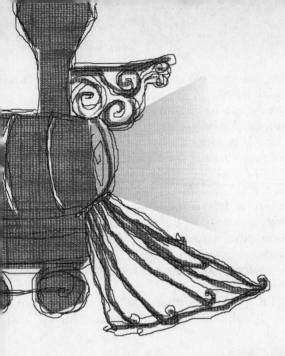

Two

When Peachy reached the spot where Danny and Duff had been, he stopped and stared around the nearly empty Covent Garden. "They were right here," he told Clair, who was standing with her arms folded in disbelief. "They were selling papers, and I went to get lunch. They said they would wait."

"How long were you gone?" Clair asked with a toss of her curls. "It could be that Duff was so hungry he just couldn't wait. Maybe they were *worried* about you."

Peachy was considering this as he was bumped from behind. He turned to see Duff looming over him. The larger boy's cheeks were bulging.

Duff said something that sounded like "Soggy Peefy." Crumbs shot out of his half-closed mouth.

"What?" Peachy asked, brushing bits of food from his shirt.

Duff chewed forcefully and swallowed an entire mouthful with one gulp. "I said, 'Sorry, Peachy.' Danny and me was hungry, so we got food. Cheerio, Miss Clair."

Clair looked very knowing, which annoyed Peachy a little. "And where is Danny?" Clair asked.

Duff looked around as if he did not realize that Danny was not with him. "Oh! I forgot." He started back the way he had come.

"Forgot what, Duff?" Peachy called as he ran after him.

"I forgot I was s'posed to carry the papers."

Peachy sighed as he and Clair trotted along. "You mean you didn't finish selling them?"

The three friends turned the corner onto Russell Street and saw Danny on the sidewalk in front of the pub, restacking a scattered pile of the afternoon extra. "Tried to do it all yourself?" Peachy asked as they strolled up beside him.

"Sorry, Danny," Duff said as he got to his knees and began collecting the papers also.

When Danny did not say anything, Duff stopped his work, looking very guilty. "It's all right, Duff," Danny said finally. "Just help me finish."

Duff exhaled in relief.

Until then, Clair had stood directly behind Danny. At his kindly spoken words she stepped out to the side. "That's the Daniel Wiggins I know."

"Clair!" Danny hopped up from the ground, scattering the top dozen papers again. "How are you? I didn't know you were here."

"I was at the underground construction site with the protest group when Peachy ran up and told me about a mystery—something about back alleys and strange, lurking figures. . . ."

"But it's all true," Peachy said, anxious to defend his lengthy absence. "I know what I saw, and something was not on the level."

"Is that where our lunch was?" Duff asked.

Peachy looked back to Danny. "I was walking past the surveyors' office on my way back from picking up the grub. I passed an alley, and there was a boy there picking up plans, or something, out the back door. It was the same boy I almost got in the shindy with about my last paper. Billy something. Remember?"

Danny nodded at the recollection. A twinkle showed in his eyes. "How do you know it wasn't a lunch order?"

"Large paper, chalky blue? And here's something dodgy. The kid gave him money, too."

Danny raised an eyebrow. "Suppose it was something illegal. What could we do about it?"

"One step at a time, Danny," Peachy said. "I followed him, and guess what? He went into where they are building the underground tunnel."

Duff finished repiling the papers and stood up next to the group.

"I'm for investigating," Clair said thoughtfully. "If it was something illegal that can be connected with the construction, there might be a way to stop the work."

"I'll go," Danny said at once. "If it will help Clair."

Peachy rolled his eyes. There was rivalry between the boys for Clair's attention, and Danny was quick. It made Peachy all the more anxious to act the leader. "Righto then, follow me. I know a shortcut back to the alley. We'll start there." He spun on his heels and tripped over the newly stacked edition, spilling himself and them all over the sidewalk.

"Haste makes waste," Danny said lightly, but with enough sarcasm to make Peachy flinch.

Peachy sighed. Why did Danny always have the upper hand? He always seemed to be the best at everything. Danny was great at following the clues to solving mysteries. He was always on the right track, and he didn't give up until he got what he wanted. And it looked like things were going that way with Clair Avery, too.

Just once Peachy wished he could be good at something.

"That's okay, Peachy," Duff said, touching his friend on the shoulder. Then Duff stooped and began gathering the papers again.

Clair, Danny, and Peachy helped, and soon they were done.

On the way back to the surveyors' office, Peachy filled in the details about what he had seen. He recounted a full description of the boy and what had passed between the boy and the clerk.

"Here's the plan," he said, when they reached the London Surveyors' Office. "I'll go in and question that clerk. I'll ask him if it's a square-rigged way to do business through the back door. I'll tell him that he'd better—"

"You'll do nothing of the sort!" Clair interrupted. "You can't walk in there, throwing your weight around! They'll toss you right back out. It's not subtle, Peachy Carnehan."

Danny laughed.

Peachy frowned. What did she mean by *subtle*? People were always telling him he was too impatient, that he needed to form a plan before acting, but they'd never used the words *not subtle* before.

"No," Clair continued. "What you need to do is tell me which clerk it was you saw, and I'll handle the matter."

Spotting a side window set high in the alley wall, Peachy removed his cap. Climbing first onto a cabbage crate, he hopped up on the ledge and slowly raised his head above the trim to see in. At first he saw no one as he looked around an office full of file cabinets, desks, and drafting tables. His nose was near the windowsill, and he could smell the years of dust that had collected there. Cobwebs swayed gently, brushing his face.

He took another quick look and spotted one desk below the window. A clerk in the office was sitting there, hard at work.

Peachy jumped down. "I've got it! The only clerk there is the one I saw. He's sitting at a desk under the window."

"Fine," Clair said. "Now watch how polite people get things done."

Dumbstruck by her sudden criticism, Peachy said nothing as Clair strolled like a lady into the office.

•••

Upon entering the office, Clair realized the mistake that Peachy had made. There were *two* desks under the window, both currently occupied. Suddenly unsure of her plan, she grew nervous as she rang the service bell that sat neatly on the oak counter.

The clerk closest to her rose and came to the counter. "May I help you?"

"Yes," Clair said in her sweetest voice. "Actually, I'm looking for a friend. We knew each other some years ago but have since lost touch."

The man exhaled a tired sigh. His expression seemed to show that he did not want to be bothered with Clair's story.

Clair noticed his boredom, but continued anyway. "I saw him again only three days ago, and he told me he was a messenger boy for a construction company, only now I can't remember which one. I'm certain he comes here to pick up plans on occasion, as that was his destination when we met last. So I was hoping—"

The clerk interrupted, "What makes you think I can help you, miss? There are many messenger boys that do the same thing all day long. Now if you'll excuse me, I am very busy."

"Oh! I can provide a very detailed description," Clair added hastily. "His name is Billy."

"Very well," the clerk conceded with resignation. "I'll try."

As Clair carefully recounted Peachy's portrait of the ruffian, she thought she saw the clerk wince. But she had to be sure.

"No," the man said at last. "I'm quite certain I have never seen a boy like that here."

"What about that man there?" Clair asked, pointing to the other office worker seated at his desk.

"No, he would not be able to help. He doesn't deal with customers."

"Why is that?"

"He's deaf. I alone handle messengers, and I'm sure I don't know one such as you have described. Now I really must return to work."

"I see," Clair said. And indeed she did see—more than the man would have wanted her to see, she guessed. "Well, thank you for your help."

She was sure now that she had been dealing with the clerk Peachy had seen. She was even more positive that he had lied about not seeing the boy.

Peachy was right. Something odd was going on—something suspicious.

●●●

"So he lied," Danny said when the amateur detectives walked away from the surveyors' office. "But what can we possibly do now?"

The Baker Street Brigade all became quiet, trying to think of their next step.

Duff, who had been trudging along, toting the stack of afternoon newspapers, suddenly stopped walking. "I'm tired of carrying the papers," he said. "Why do I carry the papers?"

"Well, Duff," Danny said, "you're the biggest of all of us. You alone are able to carry all three of our stacks."

"But I don't like it," Duff complained. "Tell me again why I don't sell papers too."

Peachy tried to soothe the larger boy. "Duff, you're an important part of the team. You're what makes the system work. See, without us selling your share, you might get taken. You know that there are some mean people out there who wouldn't give you the right money."

"I know I can't count good," Duff agreed, "but all I do all day is stand and carry, stand and carry. I want a different job."

"Duffer," Peachy began again, "I don't think you could—"

"No, wait," Danny said with a snap of his fingers. "He can have another job if he wants one."

Clair and Peachy both looked at Danny as if he were talking nonsense.

"Think about it, Peachy. What's the logical next place to look into about this mystery you've happened onto?" Danny asked.

"The work site, I suppose," Peachy replied. "But we can't get in there. I tried and got the old heave-ho."

Duff's face was excited. "Somethin' fun," he said aloud.

"I've read in the paper how, after the accidents, it's tougher to find workers for the dig," Danny explained. "Some say the tunnel is cursed or some other glocky tale. Anyway, they are hiring laborers.

They want temporary employees to dig and do simple work like that."

"Wait a minute," Peachy argued. "You don't expect Duff to be able to work without us around."

"I can do anythin' with myself," Duff fired back at Peachy. "You said I'm big. I want somethin' fun!"

"Duff is a big bloke, and strong," Danny said. "He's our ticket in."

Clair looked doubtful.

"How will he know what to look for?" Peachy asked.

"He saw the kid, Peachy," Danny explained. "You know what a memory he has. All he has to do is keep to whatever work they put him to and watch for that chap. Then when the day is over, he can just show us who the chap talked to and what he did. Why, it will only be for a few days . . . 'til we get another lead."

Peachy nodded. "If you say so," he said. "But I still don't think it's safe."

Danny looked at Peachy thoughtfully.

Peachy never seemed to think much about others. But maybe he cared more than he let on.

•••

When the Baker Street Brigade arrived again at the construction offices, Danny stood facing Duff and put his hands on his big friend's shoulders. "Here's what you say, Duff. You say you want work. Tell them how you lug papers for a living. That you heard there was a construction job, and that you can dig good. Answer any questions they have, but don't talk much. Just listen. We'll be out here when you get done."

Clair patted Duff on the back as he walked through the gate in the fence in Tottenham Court Road. Through knotholes in the fence she and Danny and Peachy could see the row of ragged men, all applying for jobs.

Duff walked to the back of the line and patted a man on the shoulder. Danny shook his head as he pictured the conversation they

were having. Duff was telling him all the things Danny had instructed him to say, except he was saying them to the wrong person.

"I told you," Peachy said, shaking his head. "It'll never work."

The man in front of Duff laughed and pointed toward the door
of the shack.

Duff soon came back outside and rejoined the group. "He told
me there was digging jobs behind horse carriages or somethin'."

"Duff," Danny said kindly, "that was just the queue of blokes
waiting for jobs, see? You have to wait in the line before you talk to
the boss."

"Why can't you come with me?" Duff asked.

"You don't have to do this," Danny said with an attack of con-
science. "But if you do, you have to do it by yourself." He knew
there was no way rail officials would take a worker who needed
help asking for a job.

"I want a different job," Duff said again, with determination.
And he headed back through the gate to rejoin the line.

●●●

Inside the gate, the line of men moved quickly. Duff thought about
the things he would say to the clerk when he reached the window.
He was afraid, because many of the men in front of him cursed when
they were turned away. He didn't like it when men cursed. Headmaster Ingram of the Waterloo Road Ragged School said that when men
cursed, they got God's attention because they were using his name.
And they weren't using it in a nice way, like Duff did, in prayer.

Just then the applicant in front of him turned around. "Oh, you
back again?"

It was the same man who had told him he could dig behind
horse carriages. Duff kept quiet.

"I can tell you that you're not going to get hired. You're a loony."
The man laughed harshly.

Again, Duff didn't reply. He just stared down at the man, who
was much shorter than him.

The man's eyes got wide as he looked Duff over, head to toe.

Then he closed his mouth and quickly turned around. That happened often to Duff. Danny had said it was because Duff was so big. To people who didn't know him, he could look scary. Duff didn't mean to look scary to the man, but he was glad the man shut up.

Duff had almost reached the front of the line when a wagonload of bricks was driven through the gate onto the job site. Something must have distracted the driver, because he let the left-rear wheel fall into a deep rut. The wagon was stuck and could not go forward, though the driver lashed at the draft horse with his whip.

"It ain't the horse's fault," Duff mumbled. Without even thinking, he left his place in line, went to the rear of the wagon, and grasped the frame. With a heave and a shove, Duff freed the wagon from the rut.

The queue of applicants broke into applause, and the man doing the interviewing came out of the shack. "What's your name?" he asked Duff.

"Duff Bernard."

The man wrote it down. "Have you worked construction before?"

"No."

"Well, no matter. You know what a shovel is, don't you?"

Duff nodded.

"You are the strongest man I've seen today," the interviewer said, "and you're hired. You start tomorrow. Take this paper to the foreman. Can you read?"

"No," Duff said, dropping his eyes.

"It says you're a digger. Do whatever the foreman tells you to do. Don't forget, six o'clock tomorrow morning. If you're late, you're out."

Duff took the paper and hurried outside. He couldn't wait to tell his friends the news and show them the paper.

•••

"We saw what happened! Congratulations, Duff," Danny said excitedly. "You'd better get back home and rest. It'll be an early day tomorrow. Clair, I'd like to meet you tomorrow. I need to see Mr. Holmes on Baker Street. Would you like to come along?"

"I would love to," she replied.

Something about the way she said "love" made Peachy's cheeks grow hot with anger.

"Why don't you come to the school at ten?" Danny asked her. "Then we can go over together." He turned to Peachy. "You won't mind taking Duff to his new job, will you, Peachy?"

"Not at all," Peachy replied through clenched teeth. But he did mind. He minded a lot. Life was just not fair, he decided.

"Well then," Danny said, "we'll be on our way. We still have to finish selling papers, and it won't be long before the lamplighters come around. No one will buy after that."

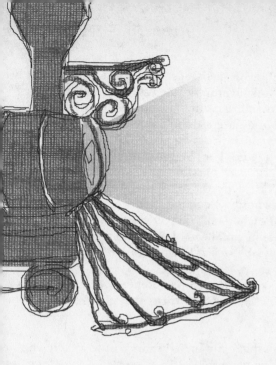

Three

Early the next morning, Peachy accompanied Duff on his way to work across the Waterloo Bridge. Beneath the nine-arched granite structure chugged a Thames River steamer, spouting a column of black smoke into the morning air. Every stroke of the engine sounded like muffled cannon fire, and it shot up puffs of steam. The cloud of smoke and steam paused on the bridge, engulfing the two friends before it swooped off above the river again in pursuit of the steamer.

"What if I don't know what to do, Peachy?" Duff was worried. "What if I don't understand?"

Peachy reached up high and patted Duff's back reassuringly. "You don't need to worry about a thing, Duff. You'll do fine. You're a hard worker. All you've got to do is work. They'll tell you how to do it."

"But that mean bloke, Peachy," Duff fretted. "I don't want no problems. That chap looked pretty angry, you know."

"Don't worry," Peachy encouraged him. "Just do what he says, and if he still gives you any trouble, then squash him like a bug."

Duff looked shocked. "Peachy! I mustn't do that!"

Peachy winked and gave a double one-two punch to the air. "Just remember that you are bigger than he is."

Duff frowned. "Righto. I am bigger than he is. . . ." *Comforting to know, but what exactly does it mean?*

He was still worried by the time they reached the Victoria Embankment on the north side of the river.

"Listen, Duff," Peachy said. "All you got to do is shovel a little dirt and take pictures in your head of what you see."

Duff gazed curiously back at Peachy. He still didn't get it. "Pictures?"

"You know—" Peachy tapped his forehead with two fingers—"remember what you see down there. Use that photographic memory of yours."

Duff nodded.

"Keep an eye on that curly-haired chavvy, Billy. Watch who he talks to. Listen to what he says," Peachy instructed. "Look for clues. You know, take pictures."

"Oh. Right. Cheerio, Peachy." Duff squinted thoughtfully at the stone obelisk of Cleopatra's Needle. "I see now."

They traveled up Wellington Street past Covent Garden. They soon reached the fenced area that concealed the excavation over the tunnel of the City and South London Railway. Because of the early hour and the frosty air, there were no protesters surrounding the site. A lone queue of men dressed in heavy denim lined up for work, stamping their feet against the cold.

"See, Duff? Look at the company you have today." Peachy stopped just short of the line. "Have you got your work card?"

Duff reached into the deep pockets of his extra-large overalls. Digging around in the bottom he discovered a button, gravel, some string, and half a hard roll saved from breakfast. Finally, there it was—a scrap of paper with a number on it. "Two-two. Here it is, Peachy."

"Good then." Peachy stuck out his hand and grasped Duff's.

"I'd better get out of here before I'm spotted. But I'll be back at five to meet you."

All these things to think about, Duff thought. How would he ever remember? "Hey, Peachy, guess what?" he called out, stopping Peachy from leaving.

"What?"

"This is my first job without you and Danny." Duff smiled big and bright-eyed, like a small child seeing the zoo for the first time.

"Congratulations, Duff. That's something that even Danny and I haven't done yet."

Duff was too proud to hold back his joy any longer. He let out a big laugh, followed by a snort.

Peachy laughed too. "Cheerio then. Look for me across the street outside the Star and Garter at five."

"Ta. See you later, Peachy." As soon as Duff got in line with the rest of the men, he forgot all of his worries. "Mornin'," he said, sticking out his hand to one of the biggest men in line. "My name is Duff. Duff Bernard."

"Pleased to meet you, Duff Bernard," the man replied kindly. "Hope they let us get to work soon and out of the this cold."

●●●

"Good morning, children." Mrs. Hudson, housekeeper to world-famous detective Sherlock Holmes, greeted Danny and Clair in her kind but slightly condescending way. "Miss Clair Avery, it's so nice to see you. Do come in."

"Thank you, Mrs. Hudson. It's nice to see you, too." Clair stepped into the front hall at 221B Baker Street.

"I'm surprised to see that your father lets you hang around this trouble," Mrs. Hudson observed, inclining her head toward Danny.

Danny smiled sweetly. "Cheers, Mrs. Hudson. Nice to see you, too."

"Mr. Holmes is in the study. Daniel, don't even think about tracking those filthy boots on my carpet!" The housekeeper made Danny remove his boots before going upstairs.

Clair was halfway up when Holmes yelled down to the door. "Mrs. Hudson! Stop patronizing my guests and bring the tea."

Danny smiled again and sprinted up the stairs.

"No running, Daniel Wiggins!" Mrs. Hudson commanded sternly before turning toward the kitchen.

"Mrs. Hudson!" Holmes screeched.

The housekeeper threw her hands in the air in frustration. In spite of her seeming irritation, Holmes and Mrs. Hudson truly appreciated each other, and Danny loved their bantering. It had to be one of the funniest things about coming over to the Baker Street flat.

When Clair and Danny entered the second-floor study, they were met by a wall of ghastly smelling purple smoke. Danny swatted his way through. He bumped into a coffee table but managed to stop a Grecian urn full of pens, knives, arrows, and blowgun darts from tipping over.

From the goggles on his head to the rubber nose clamp pinching his nostrils and the alcohol torch in his hand, Holmes had the look of a mad scientist. "Wiggins, could you open the windows, please?" He pulled back his goggles and examined a bubbling mess in an open flask.

Clair blinked as her eyes began to water from the smoke, and she covered her nose with the sleeve of her coat.

Holmes chuckled at her as he removed the nose clasp. "Good grief! I have created a devilish-smelling device, haven't I?"

While guarding his nose and mouth with one hand, Danny picked up a copy of the *Times* and began to fan the smoke out the window. "Poison gas, Mr. Holmes? I bet whatever that is would win the contest to invent a better stink bomb if you entered it."

"I'm sure you're right," Holmes agreed. "Stink-bomb contest. Is there such a thing?"

"I don't know." Danny grinned. "Maybe, but what is that anyway?"

"This, my young friends, is part of my most recent study. It is a study in forgery."

Danny nodded and rubbed his chin, staring at the molten goo in the glass container and wondering if he had heard correctly. "What does it do?"

"Aha!" Holmes snapped, flipping up his index finger. "It is—or will be, if my calculations are correct—the world's first print-lifting, copying device. As soon as it cools, we shall have a test."

"Really?" Clair exclaimed, raising her delicate eyebrows.

She and Danny stepped closer to the smoldering mess. A pinkish substance began to gel in the beaker.

"You meant to do that?" Danny exclaimed.

"Yes," Holmes agreed, taking a seat in his red-velvet armchair near the far window. He kicked his feet up on the ottoman. "So what brings you two here?"

They explained to him the incident with the bully in the square and how Peachy had seen the boy again afterward. Danny mentioned what happened at the back door of the London Surveyors' Office and was just ready to tell about the second visit to the alley when Holmes interrupted.

Holmes said in a bored tone, "Come now, Wiggins, where are your powers of deduction? If the boy was a construction worker, one who might have been down in the mud and filth, do you not find it probable that the clerk would have insisted he go around the back to pick up whatever it was he was receiving?"

Flustered by Holmes's lack of interest in the story, Danny stammered, "You see, Mr. Holmes, I thought the same thing, too, at first, but when Clair went in . . ."

Taking up the talk, Clair reported, "According to Peachy, the man I spoke with was the same one he had spotted earlier in the alley with the boy. But when I described the messenger to him, he lied. He told us that he had never seen such a boy in his life."

"Peculiar—" Holmes yawned—"but scarcely conclusive of wrongdoing. Is there more, pray?"

Danny leaned forward on the sofa. "We thought it might be connected to the recent troubles with the underground tunnel. So now we've recruited Duff to work down in the tunnel in search of any clues that might further show that something odd is going on."

Holmes thought a moment, then jumped to his feet. His nimble mind jumped subjects, too. "I believe my newest creation should be ready now." He circled the table and pulled a thin, chrome spatula from a rack of tools. The sleuth twirled the metal blade in the pink gunk and pried it loose from the beaker. The entire glob stuck to the spatula like an enormous wad of chewing gum.

"That's really strange material, Mr. Holmes," Clair observed.

The detective looked at her without comprehension, as if he did not understand her words.

"That is," she apologized, "if you don't mind my saying so."

"No, no," Holmes answered, moving the rose-colored lump back and forth in front of his face. "I'm just examining the adhesive properties that this combination seems to have. Unusual."

Holmes's invention stretched and thinned, like taffy when pulled, but could be wadded up and rolled back together in a new ball. It seemed to Danny like rubber tree sap, only not as sticky on human skin.

Grabbing a brass-nibbed pen from a holder, Holmes dipped it in an inkwell and handed it to Danny. "Will you do me the honor of signing your name here?" he asked, pointing his long, bony finger at a stack of fine stationery.

Danny agreed and inscribed his signature with a flourish. After the signing, Holmes flattened the goo into a long rectangular shape, then laid it over the sheet of paper and pressed. Slowly peeling it back revealed that a mirrored copy of Danny's name appeared on the rubbery substance.

"Yes," Holmes mumbled under his breath. "It just might work."

Clair held her hands close to her mouth in anticipation, while Danny bit his lip. Both young people watched as the critical moment arrived. Holmes laid the rubbery substance down once more and pressed it firmly against a clean sheet of paper.

Searching the eyes of Danny and Clair, the detective counted to three aloud, then slowly peeled back the substance once more. Danny leaned close to get a better glimpse, but to his deep disappointment, the experiment had not worked. The sheet of paper was pristine white, and the goo had retained the signature completely.

"Blast!" Holmes exploded. "There's nothing I hate more than wasted time!"

"I'm sorry, Mr. Holmes," Clair said sympathetically.

"Not to worry," Holmes answered in a more relaxed tone. "Science advances from experiments like these. There is no failing unless one stops before achieving the goal."

Let down by the whole event, all three occupants of the sitting-room laboratory sighed at once. Holmes crumpled up the goo and threw it at a wastebin. To his surprise, it stuck to the edge.

Danny rushed to the basket and pulled the putty off. "You're going to throw it away?"

"I've learned all I need to from that batch," Holmes said. He replaced his goggles over his eyes and fired up the burner. "I just have to keep trying until I make one that works."

"Can I have this one?" Danny blurted out. "It's interesting."

"I don't see why not," Holmes replied, glancing up from his work. "But don't eat it." The sleuth must have considered what he had said, because he looked up at Danny once more. "You wouldn't do that, would you, Wiggins?"

"No, of course not, Mr. Holmes," Danny promised. "But look," he said, molding the gunk into a ball by rolling it between his hands. "I'll bet it even bounces." Danny attempted to bounce the substance on the wood floor. It flattened slightly on impact but rebounded into his hand.

Holmes gave a satisfied grin. "Sometimes, Wiggins, you surprise even me."

Danny thanked Holmes for his new invention, and he and Clair moved toward the door.

Holmes returned to his work. But just before they stepped out, he called, "Oh, Wiggins."

"Yes, Mr. Holmes?"

"I'm sure there's nothing to it, but . . . keep me informed on your tunnel investigation, would you? There's a good lad."

"As soon as I hear anything, Mr. Holmes, you'll be the first one to know," Danny agreed and closed the door behind him. As Danny and Clair made their way down the stairs, he told Clair how wizard the new invention was.

"But what's it good for?" she wanted to know.

Danny looked thoughtful. "Don't know yet, but if it comes from the laboratory of Sherlock Holmes, it must be good for something."

●●●

Inventor and master sleuth Sherlock Holmes heard Danny's muffled words through the closed door. They made him smile.

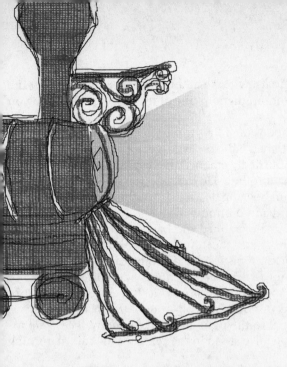

Four

"I push the barrows," Duff reported shyly to the foreman named Mr. Kelly at the door of the foreman's shack.

"Quite right," Kelly said, looking up at him. "I'm sure that's exactly what God made you for. Follow me, then. I'll show you where you'll be working today and what you're doing."

They walked to the mouth of the tunnel, which led down from the site in a gradual slope. Beyond the head of the rails, the tunnel was lined with planks on the ground for walking and shored with heavy timbers on the walls and roof. The tunnel curved, and Duff and Kelly were soon far enough in to need extra light, which was provided by dim yellow lanterns, hanging precariously from hooks.

Duff could hear heavy machinery working somewhere. It sounded like a large beast huffing and puffing in rapid rhythm. Kelly led the boy to a spot where several other men were shoveling dirt into wheelbarrows.

"Here we are," Kelly said as they stopped walking. "You are to take the full wheelbarrows, one at a time, back up the tunnel the way we came and dump them in one of the piles up there. Do you understand?"

Duff nodded and waited for the next instruction. Kelly stared at him for a moment, then barked, "Well, get to work, then."

Duff jumped, hurriedly grabbed the handles of a wheelbarrow, and shoved it to set it rolling. He followed the line of the planks to keep the wheel from bogging down in the muddy floor. Quickly he was back in the yard and dumping the load.

Duff shivered as he grabbed the handles of the wheelbarrow again and headed back into the tunnel. The dim shadows cast by the lanterns played tricks on his vision. When he came to a fork in the tunnel, he could not remember which way was correct. The noise of the drilling and hammering was no clue. It seemed to come from everywhere at once, or nowhere at all—out of the rocks themselves. Duff took the tunnel to the right and walked and walked. Perhaps he had chosen wrong. He stood in the center of the cavern, turning round and round.

"I just push the barrows," he said aloud to himself. "I just push the barrows." Duff's voice resounded hollowly. The boy did not like the way it came back to his ear with a deeper ringing tone. He leaned against a crumbling block of concrete, which left a white paste on his trouser legs. "Oh, new britches. Miss Bingham will be mad."

Duff jumped when a voice suddenly spoke to him. "What's that you say, sonny?" Around the nearest curve in the tunnel was an old man, worn down by years of hard labor.

Overjoyed at finding someone else in the dim depth, Duff ran to him.

The miner's face was pale and covered with rock dust. It seemed to Duff that in the odd, yellow light he could see the man's skull through his skin. When the tunnel worker spoke again, his voice was gravelly and hoarse. "What's your name?"

"Duff Bernard."

"Well, Duff Bernard, you are a lucky one."

"Why?" Duff asked, curious at the mysterious tone.

"Because, my boy, you are a runner."

Duff looked puzzled.

"You are one what has a job where you can see daylight. It drives you insane to be down here. It's dark when I come to work, dark all my time here, dark when I come up . . . plays tricks on your mind. When you're my age—" the wizened man paused to hack and cough—"when you're my age, the earth grabs you. It sucks you in like a grave."

Duff's mouth dropped wide-open as the old man continued. "You can stare at it, and it comes alive. The earth is angry that we pick at it, cut it, and tear it apart. It's mad, and it sucks us in. Look here." The skeletal figure swung his shovel against the side wall with sudden violence. To Duff's amazement, the blade broke through into a hollow space behind the rock.

The aged miner smashed his tool several more times in the same spot until an opening about a foot square gave access to a small recess behind the wall. Duff could see that the chamber was not just dirt, but lined with cut stones or bricks.

The old man reached in with a gnarled hand and withdrew . . . a skull. The bottom jaw was missing, and the eye sockets seemed to stare horribly.

"You see?" the miner asked. "Four hundred . . . six hundred . . . a thousand years dead? Who knows? Viking perhaps, maybe even old Roman. No matter. The earth sucked him in. He's been waiting here in the dark . . . waiting."

Duff wanted to scream.

The miner tossed the skull from one hand to the other. Then the man turned to face Duff. He held the skull so that the old miner's skeletal living face and the ancient dead one were both looking at the boy. "So run, Duff Bernard," the tunneler insisted suddenly. "Keep running and enjoy the sunshine. Someday you'll be stuck down here, too."

A very frightened Duff turned and grabbed another half-full wheelbarrow. He dashed full speed up the planks, past the fork in the line, and up to the mouth of the tunnel. No matter how far he ran, he thought he could still hear high-pitched cackling from behind him.

When he reached the top, Duff looked back over his shoulder for the hundredth time to see if anything was chasing him. When he turned forward again, he had to instantly swerve to avoid hitting a boy. The figure was about Duff's age, thinner and curly-haired. And he had a very mean look, Duff thought. In the abrupt swing to the side, the dirt spilled and scattered over the planks. Duff fell over the upturned cart.

"Clumsy!" the boy yelled. "Get up, stupid. Look what you did. You almost hit me!"

"I-I'm sorry," Duff stammered as he got to his hands and knees. He tried to put the spilled soil back, spooning it up with both hands.

"I said get up! What? Are you glocky?"

Duff obeyed and rose to his feet. *This is the boy. This is the one I'm supposed to watch for.* "The mean one," Duff finished aloud, without intending to speak.

"What was that? Are you talking about me? Listen, you," the curly-haired youth said as he walked toward Duff. The thin boy poked at Duff's chest with an outstretched finger. "You'd better watch your step around here, or I'll have my uncle fire you. Now stay here and clean some of this up while I go and get you a shovel."

Duff returned to his hands and knees to scoop up the dirt. Light from the tunnel mouth shone around him, and he felt the sun on his neck. He remembered what the strange old man had said. He did not want to stop running. He did not want the earth to suck him in.

"Bernard!" Foreman Kelly shouted behind him, making him jump. "What are you doing here?"

Duff stuttered again as he rose to his feet. "I—we had—I had an accident."

"An accident? Are you hurt?"

"No," Duff said, on the verge of tears.

"Well, no harm done. Just be careful. We don't need any more serious accidents around here, now do we?"

"Yes, sir," Duff said. "No, sir, I mean. I'll be careful." When Kelly walked away, the boy spoke to himself again. "No fun at all."

•••

It was near quitting time, about 4:30 in the afternoon. Charles Ruby, owner of Ruby Construction Company, sat in his office in the foreman's shack and gazed out the window at the enormous hole of the tunnel mouth. Leaning back in his chair, he tapped the barrel of a pen against his chin, frequently stopping to chew on the end. Occasionally he rested his heavy jaw on his palm. The size and shape of his jaw were comparable to the bow of a tugboat. It suited Ruby, who had come up from nothing and was used to shoving things out of the way or pushing people around to get them moving.

Born in grinding poverty in Whitechapel, Ruby had done about every kind of job imaginable, from sweeping at a post office to laying bricks. *What lousy jobs they were,* he remembered. All the time he wanted more. He desired to live better than the bottom rung of life's ladder on which he'd been placed. The constant striving and straining to improve his lot had given him a deep wrinkle that stretched all the way across his forehead. *But soon I won't have to struggle any more,* he thought, *if everything will just go well underground.*

The City and South London Railway was a project that had been bid on years ago. Ruby had gotten a reputation as a well-respected mining contractor. If the string of accidents and unaccountable delays did not interfere, the job would get done and Ruby would be comfortably well-off. Ruby pondered it all and finally threw the pen across the room just as there was a knock at the door.

It opened and his construction foreman, Iron Kelly, stepped in.

"How are things?" Ruby demanded. "Are we back on schedule?"

Kelly smiled and nodded. "Sure, and things are looking up. Got a bit more straightening up to do down there, but the wall is replaced. I still cannot account for how there came to be double charges in all that shot. Really, we got off easy. A mistake like that could have brought the entire ceiling down."

Refusing to be drawn into a renewed discussion about the explosion, Ruby looked back at his desk. His eyes traced the lines on a set of plans. "I've got a copy of that section right here."

Kelly pointed at a dark line. "This all had to be removed," he explained. "The concrete was almost completely green inside. It's a wonder it was holding up anything even before it busted up. Then, too, the fire in the timbers helped things none. Had to shore up another hundred feet. But now it's done," Kelly said with satisfaction. "Two days sooner than I thought." Ruby nodded but made no comment, so Kelly continued, "Listen, Mr. Ruby. I need to talk to you about the budget."

Ruby immediately became defensive. "What about it?"

"Well—" Kelly paused to find the right words—"not to question your judgment, but it seems like this job may be cutting a few corners."

"Corners!" Ruby yelled. "This is costing thousands more than I budgeted. And what with the accidents—"

They were interrupted by the door opening again. The curly-haired youth, whistling "I'll Take You Home Again, Kathleen," entered without knocking and addressed the owner. "Say, Mr. Ruby, I wanted to tell you about how I handled this slacker today."

Ruby sighed and looked away toward the window.

Iron Kelly turned to his nephew with his palms up to stop the flow of cheerful words.

"Not now, Billy. Wait outside," Ruby instructed. "I'll talk to you about it in a minute."

Evidently sensing the tension in the office and realizing his error, Billy frowned nervously and quickly left.

Once more Kelly pleaded with Ruby. "Cheaping out is a serious concern. Safety must come first."

"What are you talking about, cutting corners?" Ruby yelled, jabbing the desk with his index finger. "I've accounted for every aspect of this operation from blasting fuses to doorknobs, and I plan to get it in under the bid! You just do your job and keep the men working. I'll worry about the material."

"But that's just it," Kelly argued. "If we have any more accidents, it won't be possible to finish on time."

Slamming his fist down on his desk, Ruby announced, "It's *my* job to decide what is spent. It's *my* job to get the material. I did all that. Now it's *your* job to see that we don't have any more problems and that we come in on budget, or you can look for work elsewhere! Understand?" Ruby's pale green eyes burned with fire.

Kelly was totally subdued by Ruby's intense rage. "Yes, sir," he answered, looking at the floor.

Ruby swiveled around in his chair to face the window until Kelly stepped out, closing the office door quietly.

•••

After waiting a minute, Ruby stood up and also walked outside. Kelly, his foreman, was nowhere in sight.

The foreman's nephew stood beside the steps outside the door as Ruby slowly came down. The company owner gave the boy a quick smile. "What can I do for you?"

Looking around uneasily, Billy apologized. "Sorry I barged in like that."

"Never mind," Ruby said with a quick shake of his head. "Sometimes the boss just needs to make it clear who's in charge." He patted Billy on the back. "So you say there was a slacker down there today."

Billy cheered up. "Too right! He dumped a whole load of dirt. No problem though," the boy continued, bragging. "I straightened him out. Told him almost what you just said to my uncle in there."

"That's good." Ruby stopped to look in Billy's eyes. The owner stared directly into them, leaning his head as he spoke softly. "Keep up the good work." He raised his voice again. "Maybe you'll wind up with your uncle's job." Ruby laughed.

Billy suddenly looked uncomfortable.

"I've got big plans for you," Ruby concluded, reassuring the boy. Then, with a wink, Ruby walked off toward the gate.

•••

Duff followed the other workers toward the tunnel entrance as the giant steam whistle sounded, signaling the end of a long day's work. The tired, sore, and dirty workmen filed one after another to the front gates of the site. Most were heading to their favorite pub, then to a small bed in a tiny house, only to awaken early the next day to repeat the experience. On and on it went for the miners, given variety only by their restful Sundays, the single free day they were allowed per week.

Duff was now convinced that other jobs were no more fun than selling newspapers. He wished he were standing, holding the stack of papers again with his friends, Danny and Peachy. As he trudged toward the entrance he wiped a dirty hand across his face, rubbed his tired eyes, and left a streak of mud on his nose and right cheek.

Glancing at the foreman's shack, Duff noticed the curly-haired boy and Kelly standing together. Then the boy ran toward the opposite end of the work yard. Duff paid little conscious attention, but his mind filed away the connection between the boy and Foreman Kelly. Without his being able to explain it, Duff could often recall events, pictures in perfect detail. Sherlock Holmes had found that ability very useful on several occasions.

Duff was so tired, however, that he barely noticed Peachy standing in the appointed spot.

Peachy grabbed his arm. "Cor blimey, Duff! You look like you've just been dug out yourself. Look at your face. Like one of those Egyptian mummies at the British Museum. And just look at that muck on your trouser leg."

"I'm tired," Duff said simply, feeling the ache in the bottom of his feet. "I don't like this job."

"I know it's tough. But you only have to keep it up for a week. Then you can come back to selling papers with us if you want. Even less time if we crack this case."

Thinking about the long week ahead made Duff miserable. He could feel tears in his eyes.

Peachy looked down, as if he felt bad for Duff, too. Then Peachy asked, "Did you see the boy again?"

Duff sniffed and wiped his face with his forearm, turning the dust into mud. "Yes. I saw him twice. He's not a nice person, Peachy. And the second time he was with a man."

Peachy got excited. "Who was he with, Duff? Was it the boss?"

"I guess so." Duff shrugged. "It was him right there." Duff pointed to Kelly, the foreman.

"Who's that?" Peachy demanded, after sizing up Kelly's work clothes. That figure did not look like a scheming criminal. "Some workman?"

"No, that's Mr. Kelly, my foreman. He's nice, but that boy's his nephew, and I don't like him at all."

Peachy stared at his feet. "So it's the foreman's nephew, is it? I wonder what he's up to. Come on, Duff. Let's go find Clair and Danny right away. I think they'll want to hear this."

●●●

As Peachy and Duff walked, Peachy thought things over. Perhaps he *had* been too hasty in his deduction after all. A foreman *might* be up to something.

●●●

In the upstairs dormitory of the Waterloo Road Ragged School, the lights were out except for one shaded lamp. The sounds of boys sleeping, with their varying sighs, moans, grunts, and snores, filled the air.

As often happened at the end of an interesting day, no matter how tired they were, Danny and Peachy could not sleep without a final conversation. Tonight was no exception.

In their curtained cubicle, Peachy and Danny reviewed Duff's experiences. "I don't think we know much more now than we did," Danny commented. "A crazy old man is just that . . . crazy, not wicked. And I don't think there's anything to that curse business, just because of some old bones."

"What about that bloke Billy being the foreman's nephew? That's important," Peachy commented.

"Yes, but we still don't know that they are up to something. In fact, that connection means there are good reasons for Billy to carry plans back to the job."

Peachy shook his head. "Don't forget the clerk and the alley. Duff did well today," he added. "Poor chap . . . he's knackered. Just about done in. Danny, do you ever wonder why some people seem to have everything, and others . . . like us . . ." Peachy paused. "Well, not that we don't have anything, but besides each other and the school, we really don't have much. And we have to work hard always."

Danny lay on his cot, quietly pondering Peachy's question. He stared at the timbers and the cracks in the boards of the ceiling. "I guess some people are born with a lot. But by hard work we can make something of ourselves, Peach, don't you think?"

Peachy rolled to his side to face Danny. He leaned on his elbow and rested his head on his hand. "I can think of all these things that I want to do with my life. Only they don't stay the same long enough for me to reach one of them."

"I know what you mean. One day I wanted to be a circus performer so I could see the world and be famous, and the next I wanted to work with that French bloke, uh, Marey." Danny turned to face Peachy. "You know, the French chap with the moving-picture gun. I'd love to learn how to make photographs that almost come alive."

"That would be wizard," Peachy agreed. "But how do you get to?"

"Headmaster Ingram says any goal takes prayer, passion, practice, and persistence," Danny answered confidently. "*Prayer*, so God can let you know if you are on the right track. Otherwise, the other steps are a waste of time. *Passion*, because you have to want it a lot. *Practice*, because you won't be turned into something by magic, and *persistence*, meaning you have to work, and work hard, till you get where you want to be. Everyone wants to be the best at something. What do you want to do, Peach?"

"I was waiting for you to ask." Peachy chuckled. "That's my problem! Sometimes I think I want to be the editor of a big newspaper, and sometimes I want to be a missionary, like my folks . . .

and sometimes I just want to run away and be a sailor. That sounds exciting, doesn't it?"

"It does." Danny nodded thoughtfully. "But you know what it sounds like to me?"

"What's that?"

"I think you need a plan," Danny said as he rolled flat on his back to see his thoughts projected on the ceiling beams. "You must think of what you want to do and work backward through the steps to get there. Like being an editor. If you want to be that, then first you gotta be a reporter. And before that, you have to know how to write. And before you can write really good, you gotta be able to read."

Peachy frowned as if he were offended. "I can read."

"See"—Danny reinforced his thought—"you're already part of the way there! But if you couldn't read very well, then you'd have to learn, and you would, if being an editor is something that you really wanted to do."

When Peachy sighed, Danny knew he'd gotten through to his friend. So he continued, "Thinking backward like that really helps me know what I have to do next. I set goals, small ones and big ones, and I pray about 'em. With God's help, I believe I can be whatever I set my sights on. Anything!"

Peachy looked astonished. "Where did you learn all that?"

Danny laughed. "Oh, I guess I just listened in chapel. Headmaster Ingram talked about what the Bible says in Jeremiah. It goes something like this: 'I know the thoughts I think toward you, says the Lord, thoughts of peace and not of evil, to give you a future and a hope.' Now I figure that if God already has plans for me, then what I most need to do is find out what they are."

A minute of silence passed after the discussion.

Finally, Peachy sighed. "Enough about the future. We gotta figure out this case."

"I know. I feel sorry for Duff. He's out there breaking his back at six in the morning." Danny looked at Duff, sound asleep and snoring. The large boy was lying on his face, with his thumb in his mouth and his rear in the air. Danny chuckled softly. "Oy, Peachy, look at Duff."

Peachy looked and snorted. Snickering while trying to keep quiet, he whispered, "It gives a whole new meaning to sleeping like a baby."

Danny laughed again but was concerned for their friend. "They are working him pretty hard. Did you see his clothes?"

"I know—caked with mud and gunk," Peachy noted, seeing Duff's overalls hanging over a chair. "Danny, look!"

"Shh, you'll wake the others." Danny sat up in bed. "What?"

Peachy pointed. "Look at the holes in his britches!"

"Something burned holes all over them!" Danny exclaimed. He jumped from his bed for a closer look.

"What could do that?"

"I don't know. I've never seen anything like it. The material is just gone, and it looks burned." Danny reached to feel the ragged edges of the burned spots.

"Don't! It could be dangerous," Peachy insisted. "If something did that to the trousers, think about what it would do to your fingers."

"We should take these to Mr. Holmes tomorrow. He'll be able to figure it out."

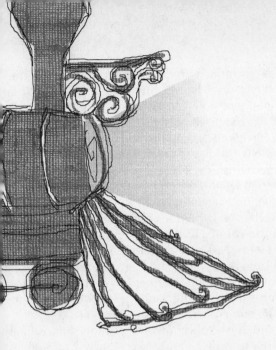

Five

Baker Street was bustling with activity on the frosty morning. Double-decker omnibuses jammed with shop clerks on their way to work crowded the intersection at Marylebone Road. The breath of the draft horses made plumes of steam from their nostrils, as if they were fire-breathing steeds from some medieval myth. The passengers, wrapped in layers of coats and capes and muffled up to their eyes in scarves, probably wished the horses could breathe fire—anything to warm up the frigid London street.

All the way from Waterloo Road Ragged School, good humor and good companionship had been the fuel to warm Danny and Peachy's morning . . . or at least to speed up the time. Danny roared with laughter as he shut Sherlock Holmes's front door behind him. "I can't believe we dropped Duff off for work in Leonard Shomar's pants."

"I know." Peachy chuckled as they climbed the stairs. "His big ankles were shining bright white like a fresh-painted fence!"

"And the look on his face when he put them on."

"He frowned like somebody gave him a big bite of lemon!"

The two friends continued to laugh hilariously until they reached the top of the stairs. Then Danny patted the air with an outstretched hand. "Silence now." In his other hand he carried a bundle of rags with the damaged overalls rolled up inside. Peachy fought back a smile, then knocked on the door.

"Come in," Sherlock Holmes instructed sharply.

When they entered the study, Peachy could still feel his freckled cheeks glowing red from laughter.

Holmes was seated in his reading chair in the corner. The consulting detective peered from behind his spectacles over the top of a book bound in maroon-colored leather. "Sunburned in the middle of winter, Peachy?" Holmes asked with a smile.

First Peachy snorted, then Danny did likewise, and before long they were both in an uproar again. Holmes lowered the book to a round end table on his left. Then, flicking his legs down from the footstool, he stood up and walked around to a tea cart.

Peach wrestled with the recollection of Duff's appearance, finally sobering up enough to provide an answer. "Sorry, Mr. Holmes. It's not a sunburn. It's just that Duff looked so funny in these pants that were too short."

"It sounds droll," Holmes said, raising an eyebrow, "but spare me the details. I hate to squirt tea from my nose so early after my bath. Please sit. Tea and rolls for you two?" he asked, holding up the silver pot and serving tray.

"Yes, please," they both said simultaneously.

Holmes passed the tray over to them. "Today's selection is gingerbread and buttered scones."

"Thanks, Mr. Holmes." Danny set the bundle down between his feet before gratefully taking one of the toasted currant-filled scones. The warm pastry dripped melted butter.

"Mighty posh of you, Mr. Holmes," Peachy added, selecting a generous square of spicy-smelling dark cake. "Gingerbread is my favorite."

"Ah, good then," Holmes responded, pouring two more cups of tea. "Cream and sugar?"

"Both for both of us, I think," Danny told him.

Peachy nodded happily, his mouth full of cake.

Holmes dropped two sugars in each cup, poured a dab of cream, and stirred. He carried the tea to them, then retreated to his armchair by the coal fire. "So what brings you gentlemen here so bright and early?"

Peachy finished a sip. "Well," he began, looking over at the bundle on the floor, "in that bundle is the strangest thing me and Dan have ever seen."

Holmes looked on curiously. "Really?" the sleuth commented dryly. "What is it?"

"Duff's work pants," Peachy continued. "When we picked him up yesterday, he had this pasty white stuff all over the legs of his pants."

"Yes. Do go on," Holmes said thoughtfully.

Danny picked up the bundle and began to unfold it.

"Danny and I were talking," Peachy explained, "and I looked over and saw big holes in Duff's pants. And they weren't there when he went to work."

Holmes got up out of his chair quickly and walked toward the pants for a closer look.

Danny showed him the holes. "It struck me funny because it looks like they'd been burned or something, but there's no smell of smoke."

The detective's long, thin nose crinkled as he sniffed the tattered places. "Acid," Holmes diagnosed immediately. "Did you touch this?" he asked, taking the piece of clothing over to his lab table.

Danny shook his head.

Holmes snipped a bit of ragged cloth and placed it under a microscope. "I can see some of the white residue that you spoke of, and it looks as though the acid is still active. The chalky substance appears to be of cement powder, but it's been completely broken down in the reaction." Holmes searched a bit further. "Where did he get this?"

Peachy sat forward to reply. "He said he fell down and got the white mud on him down in the tunnel. Said he got lost and was a long way from the rest of the workmen, except for one crazy old man."

Holmes looked up at them with concern. "Has Duff complained of any itching or irritation on his legs?"

"No. I think he took off the overalls before the holes burned through."

"Good." Holmes resumed his study. "Few chemists in town carry an acid of this potency. So the first order of business is to determine its strength."

"And that will tell us the uses and possibly lead us to the source of the acid?" Danny interjected.

"Correct, Wiggins," Holmes agreed. "And in order to reach that objective, I'll need to perform a simple test, which is similar to mixing baking soda and vinegar." He put on his lab goggles and protective rubber gloves. "You know that acids and their opposites, called bases, react with each other. That reaction explains why vinegar, which is an acid, causes baking soda, a base, to bubble and fizz. The process liberates bubbles of the gas, carbon dioxide. Now, I have here," he said, taking down two glass bottles of colored liquids, "liquids that are known to react to the presence of acid, and in precisely known ways."

"May I see one of those bottles?" Danny asked.

"Certainly," Holmes agreed, handing over a small jar containing an aqua-colored substance. "This is thymal blue. If it comes in contact with an acid, it will change color to red or yellow. The stronger the acid, the brighter the color."

"How do you explain stronger when it comes to an acid?" Peachy wanted to know.

"Quite the right question, Carnehan. Acids and bases are measured on a scale from zero to fourteen, called the pH scale. Zero is the strongest acid, fourteen the most powerful base. Thymal blue reacts to acids stronger than a pH of 2.8 and can indicate strength down to a pH of 1.2. Watch." Holmes took the bottle back from

Danny and placed a few drops in a small glass beaker. Using twee-
zers, he carefully plucked a bit of the white substance and dropped
it into the beaker. The solution changed immediately to a brilliant,
angry yellow. "Just as I suspected," Holmes announced. "It is stronger than 1.2."

"So what do we do now?" Peachy asked, completely absorbed
in the experiment. "Is that the best we can do?"

"Not at all," Holmes reassured the boy. "This bottle"—he flourished a second vial containing a yellow-green fluid—"is methyl
green. Watch again." This time, when Holmes added the suspicious
substance to the indicator liquid, it became a brilliant blue.

"What does that mean, Mr. Holmes?" Danny inquired.

"It means danger, Wiggins," Holmes said. "That color only
appears when the acid is 0.2 pH . . . one of the strongest acids I have
ever seen. And notice, gentlemen, this is *after* some of its potency
has been neutralized by the cement. Working backward tells us that
when the acid was first applied, it was extremely powerful, capable
of eating into concrete."

Danny nudged Peachy's arm. "See, working backward from the
objective is the plan even in detective work."

"Now, if you'll bear with me, boys," Holmes said, "I want to
conduct further tests that will tell me more."

The boys drank tea and ate scones while watching Holmes as
he carried out his experiments. Before they even knew it, close to
two hours had passed. The results were ready, but not until Holmes
had completed his math, checked it, recalculated, and checked it
again.

Holmes lifted his goggles quietly and stared at the door, as if in
a daze. He did not say a word.

Danny and Peachy grew concerned.

"Mr. Holmes?" Peachy asked. "Uh, Mr. Holmes, are you all
right?"

At first the master sleuth did not move or blink. Then he said
slowly, "Yes." He looked at the boys. "Yes, everything is fine, but I
almost don't believe my findings."

"What?" the boys coaxed. "What is it?"

Holmes restudied his work as he explained. "Based on the hypothetical time frame I have allowed, no acid I possess is strong enough to last. But this acid is so strong that not only have I never used it, but I can hardly believe anyone else in Britain has either . . . until now. . . ." His eyes took on their previous faraway look. "They had to have received it on the black market."

Peachy cocked his head to one side. "Black market, Mr. Holmes? What makes you think that?"

"Because, my dear boy, I have only read about an acid of this strength once before." Holmes launched into his tale with animation. "It was almost four years ago, in my *Journal of Science* monthly. It was an acid demonstrated to other scientists that had the power to make metal as soft as clay. In fact, it would turn concrete into a paste in a matter of minutes."

Danny and Peachy hovered attentively on the edge of their seats.

"The chemical mixture, a form of hydrofluoric acid, was created by a German scientist who spent several years working on the project." Holmes rubbed his forehead, blinking his tired eyes. "Soon after the demonstration, but before the chemist published his findings, a group of men broke into his basement laboratory and stole all of the remaining chemical along with the plans." Holmes stared into the empty gray light of the window, and his breathing seemed to quicken. "The scientist apparently encountered the burglars in the act. He was found many days later, tied in a chair, dead." Holmes turned to the boys and whispered with horror in his voice, "They used the acid on him."

Peachy felt sick to his stomach. He wished that he had not eaten all that gingerbread. Danny looked pale, as if he was queasy, as well.

"That circumstance provides all the necessary reason to take this case very seriously. Someone will stop at nothing to prevent the completion of the tunnel."

Peachy shivered from the thought. "So you think the murder and the trouble with the underground are connected?"

"Connected, most definitely. However, are they one and the same criminal mind? I cannot say. Never run faster than the facts lead. Come, Wiggins, we must ready ourselves for a mission."

"But where are we going?" Danny asked. He appeared dazed.

"To the construction site, as a building inspector and his helper," Holmes announced, swooping across the room to open the linen closet door. "Peachy? You've been seen at the tunnel already, have you not?"

"I have, and been thrown out as well."

"As I remembered. I don't think it would be a wise decision to take you along. However, if you would meet us at the protesters' meeting tonight at the Whitefield church, I'm sure we'll have more to discuss."

"Of course, Mr. Holmes. Good luck to you." Peachy stretched out his hand to Danny.

The two friends shook firmly. Just as Danny opened the door for Peachy's departure, Holmes's arm stretched into sight from behind the closet door. He was holding a suit of clothes. "Wiggins, put this on. The game is afoot!"

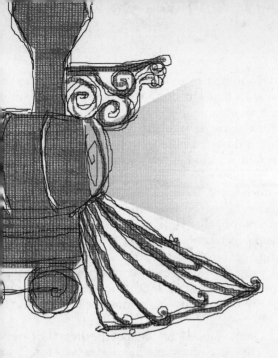

Six

Danny pulled a scratchy starched collar away from his neck as the cab rounded the corner onto Oxford Street. "Mr. Holmes," he said plaintively, "are you sure this is necessary?"

Holmes glanced over. His face had completely changed. He now seemed like a total stranger, which still frightened Danny a little. "Yes, Wiggins. Very necessary. Do you think they would let Sherlock Holmes in if they were trying to conceal something? No, today I must be Archibald Fairaday, building inspector."

"But why would they let an inspector in and not you? As yourself, I mean."

"Because, my boy, when Sherlock Holmes calls, it's obvious he is searching for signs of foul play. But they cannot refuse Mr. Fairaday, or they would incur the wrath of the entire London City Building Council. At this point they cannot afford any more setbacks."

Danny did not like the setup and hated the way Holmes referred to himself as "Sherlock Holmes," as if he really were someone else.

Danny also disliked Holmes's new look. The supposed Fairaday was fat-featured, his cheeks stuffed with cotton, his nose lumpy because of being covered in strange skin putty.

Holmes had added to the realistic disguise by pasting on bushy brown eyebrows and a droopy mustache that passed his chin in length. He even stuffed his clothes with extra bulk and wore a brown wig.

The only thing unchanged, Danny noticed, was Holmes's set of sharp eyes. The detective's gaze seemed to pierce the skulls of everyone and read their very thoughts. *Anyone who really knows Holmes,* Danny thought, *would recognize him from those eyes.*

"Remember, Wiggins," Holmes blurted out, snapping Danny out of his thoughts, "you are my page. My errand boy. For this disguise to work properly, you must be that person. Do what I say, when I say, or even the most dumb of criminals will see through us."

"I'll remember." Danny yanked the collar of the dress shirt away from his neck again. He also disliked the disguise he was forced to wear—a blue suit, the fibers of which scratched him, and a small, round cap, whose black leather chin strap irritated him. He carried an attaché case for Holmes, the contents of which were unknown.

The shiny, black hansom cab stopped jerkily up the street from the gates of the construction site, as Tottenham Court Road was filled with protesters. "I'm sorry, sir," said the cabbie from his perch up behind. "This is as close as I get."

Mr. Fairaday and his page disembarked after paying the driver. Holmes, the now building inspector, strutted confidently to the gate as the demonstration temporarily stopped to let them pass. People seemed mesmerized by the inspector's air. As he banged on the wooden gate, all chanting came to a halt.

"What do you want?" The voice that came from within was hostile. "If this is a trick, we'll arrest the lot of you."

Holmes adopted a pompous attitude, mimicking a London bureaucrat. "I am Archibald Fairaday, building inspector. Due to growing concern over reported accidents, this site has been chosen for a surprise inspection." The detective sniffed in an arrogant way. "Open up at once."

The crowd cheered, hoping that this would mean the end of the dangerous tunneling under their businesses, homes, and churches.

Overwhelmed by the information, the guard stuttered. "I . . . I . . . well, yes, sir. Please follow me." The watchman rolled back the gate and closed it behind them, leading Holmes and Danny to the foreman's shack.

"You see, sir," the guard said to Holmes, "it might be difficult to arrange. Mr. Ruby's the contractor, but I suppose you already know that. Well, Mr. Ruby's away at a different site today. The foreman, Mr. Kelly, is here, but I don't know if he has the authority—"

Holmes interrupted. "He doesn't need any authority. I am here with the law behind me and will inspect the site with or without your cooperation."

The guard swallowed hard and nodded briskly.

They entered the shack without knocking and found Kelly sitting behind his desk, almost hidden in back of mountains of paperwork. He rose as they filed in.

"Mr. Kelly," the guard stammered, "a Mr. Archibald Fairaday. He's a building inspector, come on a surprise visit."

Kelly thanked the guard and motioned for him to leave. "Please sit down, Mr. Fairaday. I'm sorry Mr. Ruby isn't here, but I'm sure I can oblige your request. We want to cooperate every way we can. Since I'm sure Henry checked your credentials thoroughly, I won't ask for them again. But I do need one thing."

Danny felt a pang of fear shoot through his stomach.

"What is that?" Holmes asked as flatly as he could.

"I need you and your aide to sign release forms. It's required of all visitors."

"Why, yes. Of course."

Kelly opened a file-cabinet drawer and pulled out a folder. He removed one paper and retrieved a black fountain pen from the drawer. Danny tried to think of an alternate name for himself, as he knew Holmes would be signing Archibald Fairaday. *Do they know my name?* he wondered. *Best not take any chances if someone looks at this later. Daniel Dravot,* he thought, *that's easy enough.*

When Holmes handed him the pen, Danny leaned over the paper and signed the pseudonym as best he could. He allowed his eyes to drift to the signature above his. There, signed in a beautiful script, was the name Sherlock Holmes. Danny panicked. He thought about scribbling it out, but that would be too suspicious.

Holding the pen up in his right hand and the paper in the other, he showed Holmes the signatures, while blocking them from Kelly's view. "Is this in order, Mr. Fairaday?" he asked. He saw Holmes's eyes go wide for a moment, just before Danny squeezed the filling lever of the pen, causing it to leak ink all over the paper.

"Oh, clumsy lad!" Holmes scolded. "Now we shall have to sign another."

"No matter," said Kelly. "I have hundreds."

This time Holmes formulated the prissy signature of Archibald Fairaday. Danny just repeated his chosen alias and congratulated himself for saving the day. It seemed the great detective Sherlock Holmes needed him after all.

Outside the little building, Danny saw the yard full of workmen and hoped that they would not come upon Duff. One never knew what Duff recognized or not. He might notice Danny and spoil the disguise.

They followed Kelly into the dim, brown tunnel past track layers, masons, and carpenters. "Where would you like to start, sir?" Kelly asked as they walked.

"I would like to see the structure that failed, causing the last accident."

Kelly nodded and walked on. Danny glanced to the right and saw a group of men digging out some rubble and Duff waiting for the diggers to fill another wheelbarrow. Danny quickly turned his head away so he would not be recognized.

"Here we are," Kelly said as they walked into a large, expansive chamber at the end of the passageway. They saw in front of them a large pile of debris that reached clear to the ceiling. Splintered timbers and the remains of concrete pillars were obviously at the root of the collapse. "That's where the structure failed."

Holmes walked forward, maneuvering his now-pudgy body toward the concrete stubs. "Wig—," Holmes began, then caught himself.

"Beg pardon, Mr. Fairaday?" Kelly queried.

"Hmmm, nothing. Dravot, bring my bag."

Danny obeyed, and Holmes unfastened the bag, rifling wildly through the contents like a child destroying a beautiful wrapping job on a Christmas present.

Kelly winced.

"Aha!" Holmes shouted as he withdrew a fine surgeon's scalpel from the case and flourished it in the air like a sword.

Danny jumped backward a little.

Holmes also scooped up a magnifying glass from the bag and approached the crumbled mortar.

Peering through the glass and taking thin swipes at the concrete with the knife, the sleuth obtained several samples, which he placed in a jar back in his bag. "It is as I had suspected," Holmes told Kelly. "This concrete was much too green to have been released from the forms. It is still several days from being completely cured."

Danny was impressed. Holmes not only acted like an arrogant building inspector, he knew the language, too.

Kelly just nodded as though the information was old. "I realize that, sir. We have been short on time since the project began, and now it seems we are short on money, too. The city is pressing for the job to be completed, the protesters want it stopped, and every time—"

"Please," Holmes said. "I am not here to listen to a catalog of excuses. I suggest work be slowed to a pace that permits proper procedure, or this site will be condemned until further notice."

"I know, sir. Believe me, I understand. I've tried to relay that same information to Mr. Ruby several times over the past weeks."

"It is as much your responsibility as his, Mr. Kelly." Holmes sounded like a lecturing schoolmaster. "Now I should like to have a look around without your hovering presence. Any results I find will be noted in my report, of which this firm will receive a copy."

"I'm sorry, sir. I can't allow—"

"I will hear no argument, Mr. Kelly." Holmes turned away and began walking back up the tunnel. "Come along, Dravot. We have much work to do."

Kelly, evidently seeing no point in arguing with the arrogant inspector, turned back to examine the rubble. He sighed, then kicked the pile, scattering rocks all over. The sound echoed loudly in the empty chamber. Then he left.

Danny waited until they had turned several curves of the tunnel before posing the question that was uppermost in his mind. "Was there acid in the concrete?"

"Weren't you listening?" Holmes shrugged. "I said it was too fresh. There wasn't even a trace of the kind of dissolution that was present in the other sample. Let us go to the area where workmen are clearing. I need to go there and find a sample."

"What about me?" Danny protested.

"What about you? I just said to come along."

"No, I mean, Duff is there. If he recognizes me, what will happen then?"

"Perhaps you're right. You'd better wait outside while I inspect the area. By the way, that was quick thinking back there with the signatures."

Danny went back to the mouth of the tunnel. He stood near piles of dirt and rock from the diggings.

"Excuse me," a familiar voice said from behind him.

No, no, no, Danny thought. He knew it was Duff.

"Excuse me," Duff repeated.

Danny tried to step out of the way without turning around, but it was no use. Duff recognized him.

"Danny? Is that you? Oh, Danny, I'm glad to see you." Duff dropped the handles of the laden wheelbarrow and ran to bear-hug Danny. Duff squeezed and lifted Danny off the ground.

"No, Duff! Don't!"

"Danny!" Duff repeated, obviously not listening to Danny's protest. "I hate work here. I hate it. You came to take me—"

"Hey, you!" Another voice boomed from across the yard. "What the devil?" Charles Ruby stormed from the foreman's shack toward the two boys.

Duff dropped Danny flat.

"Duff," Danny pleaded. "I'm not Daniel Wiggins. I'm not Daniel Wiggins. I'm Daniel Dravot, an errand boy. You have to say you don't know me. I'm Daniel Dravot."

Ruby drew nearer.

"But, Danny," Duff argued, "you're my friend Danny Wiggins."

Ruby was almost to them.

"No, Duff, listen. I'm Daniel Dravot, an errand boy for Archibald Fairaday, the building inspector."

"But, Danny," Duff persisted.

Ruby arrived at the group. "What's going on here?"

Danny spoke up, "My name is Daniel Dravot, sir. I'm the page to Mr. Archibald Fairaday, the building inspector."

Duff held his forehead in confusion. He looked hurt, too. "But, Danny—"

"So what were you doing with him?" Ruby asked Duff. "Do you know him?"

Duff tried to remember what Danny had said.

"I asked you a question." Ruby glared at Duff.

Holmes emerged from the tunnel mouth. "Daniel!" he yelled. "I've finished my work now. We can leave."

"Answer me!" Ruby demanded.

"Oh, Dravot!" Holmes called again.

Staring up at Duff, Danny saw him recognize Holmes's voice. *Oh no*, Danny thought, *this will be the end of all of it.* But then Danny noticed another look on Duff's face as his big friend turned to look for Holmes. A twinge of comprehension sharpened Duff's eyes.

"I said—," Ruby began again, but Duff cut him off.

"I knocked him down," Duff said, sticking a dirty thumb against Danny's chest. "I was just picking him up."

"You knocked him down!" Ruby was enraged.

"It's my fault, sir." Danny joined in the story. "I was standing where I shouldn't have been. He couldn't have seen me."

"And who are you again?" Ruby demanded.

"He is my assistant," Holmes said, approaching the group. "And I am Archibald Fairaday, building inspector."

Ruby instantly changed his attitude. "Mr. Fairaday. How good it is of you to visit our site. I'd quite gotten used to dealing with Mr. Patrick. Where is he this fine day?"

"It is apparent that Mr. Patrick has not been doing his job!" Holmes preached. "And in light of the recent accidents, Mr. Patrick may not be back to this site again! What is more, since he may be subject to disciplinary proceedings, I'll thank you to say nothing to him of my call."

Ruby gulped. "If there's anything I can do for you to help your inspection, please let me know. We are as anxious as the city or anyone else to see the rest of this construction be trouble free."

Holmes sniffed, as if he doubted every word Ruby said. "I have all the information I need. Good day."

Ruby turned from them disgustedly and marched back to the foreman's shack.

Danny patted Duff on the back as he and Holmes headed toward the gate.

Seven

The activity under the city of London was finished for the day. All the workers had gone home. Now life was refocused on other areas. Pubs sprang to life, theatre footlights were turned up, and gas lamps in dining establishments and private homes were lighted in preparation for supper. Lastly, the Whitefield Tabernacle at Tottenham Court Road was filling with visitors. Some were already angry, others concerned, and some merely curious.

Many people who rarely attended church were present this evening to voice their worry about the tunneling beneath the city. Almost all the seats in the great auditorium were taken up with the protestors of the underground development.

Holmes and Danny waited on the steps for Clair, Duff, and Peachy to arrive before filing in and taking seats in the last row. "So there was no trace of the acid?" Danny asked about Holmes's earlier investigation.

"No, Danny," Holmes replied thoughtfully. "What Duff discovered may have been only a test of the chemical. So we don't know who tested it or how they got it. And, more worrisome, we don't know what they intend to do with it next. For now we must turn our attention to this meeting. Watch the reactions of the audience. We may see something useful."

The discussion was chaotic. People yelled their differing opinions on how to stop the action of the tunneling. These suggestions ranged from peaceful protesting to firebombing.

It was because of this aspect of fanaticism that Holmes was present, sitting quietly unrecognized and listening to all the speakers. He had his eyes closed and his hands folded in front of him, as if his mind were a thousand miles away. But Danny knew Holmes was listening to every word and every inflection of anger or outrage.

The uproar finally stilled when Reverend Mitchell Henry walked to the pulpit. "Ladies and gentlemen," he began, "we are here to discuss the growing concern over the digging beneath our streets. This very church has been shaken at times so badly that the cross fell from the wall behind me. It is my feeling that not only the tunneling but the planned operation of trains in this area may prove hazardous to this neighborhood. Action must be taken, but what can we do?"

The crowd began shouting solutions again. Henry waited until they had quieted once more. "Please, that was rhetorical. I realize that you all have very different opinions on what should take place, but in order for our cause to be realized we must band together in one unit for one purpose. Tonight we should hear all opinions, one at a time. Then we should poll the group and put into action the plan with the most support. Please, as there are so many of us here, if you are in favor of something that has already been mentioned, say so and allow us to move on. I will recognize each of you in turn, starting with you, sir."

The reverend pointed to a well-dressed, olive-skinned man in tan trousers and a cutaway coat.

The man stood nervously and looked around the church. "My name is Bernardo Martinez. I own a shop very near here and directly above the tunnel. I sell housewares, and over the past few weeks, the blasting has gotten so bad that I have lost nearly a quarter of my stock. Dishes broken, mirrors . . . one morning an entire hutch fell over and shattered, leaving not one piece whole within. I think we need to form a line at the gates to keep workers from entering the site. I think no more work should be done until the government meets with us to study our concerns." He sat down, and the volume of conversation rose.

"And what happens when the police come to take us away?" shouted one angry man.

"That contractor Ruby is no good," yelled a woman. "I can't believe he would put his own church and family plot at risk, just for the money."

Henry spoke again and made quieting motions with his hands. "Good people, please! One at a time. We will vote on the ideas later. Now you, sir." He pointed to the lean, dark-bearded man who had shouted out against Martinez's idea.

The man rose from his seat. "My name is Randall Hanson. The time has come and gone for these peaceful protests."

Holmes's eyes narrowed, and he perked up in his seat to listen closely.

Hanson continued, "We have stood at their gates and shouted long enough, yet work continues inside. What we need is more direct action. I suggest we burn the site. The equipment, the materials, the existing structure. They can't work if there is nothing to work with."

Most of the church was silent after Hanson's comments, but he did seem to have a small following sitting near him, who verbally agreed.

Reverend Henry wiped his forehead before returning to the pulpit. "So we have heard the two most opposing methods of response. Are there any more plans of attack?"

Some attendees chuckled at the reverend's joke. Hanson just glared.

Holmes stood from his seat in the back. "Before I decide which way to vote," he said, "I should like to have a man of the cloth's opinion on both. What do you say, Reverend Henry?"

Many in the church nodded their agreement, so Henry decided to speak. "I have seen a great many religious battles in my day. I have found that only one method will win the support of the general public. People who don't have your passion for the cause, Mr. Hanson, would call you an extremist and would not support your case in any form. Indeed, violent actions beget only more violence and drive otherwise sympathetic people away."

Hanson was visibly upset, but Henry continued. "I happen to agree with that assessment. Think of what happens when such action is taken. Work is delayed for a period of time, be it six months, a year, or maybe just a week. You would end up in jail, and the general public would look upon all of us as fanatical fools and turn away. I ask you, Mr. Hanson, what good does that plan of action do our cause, the church, or you?" He paused before answering his own question. "Nothing."

Hanson rose and stormed down the aisle to the rear of the church, slamming the door behind him. Some of his followers rose slowly and exited, but others stayed.

Reverend Henry concluded his speech. "In my opinion, there is no place in the civilized world, church, or state for such fanatics. In the words of the Master, 'Be wise as serpents *and* harmless as doves.' Shall we vote?"

●●●

Outside the church, Holmes spoke quietly to Danny. "We know now who may be responsible, should anything tragic occur again. I must investigate this fellow Hanson. Miss Avery?" He turned to where Clair was talking to Peachy and Duff. "Miss Avery, Reverend Henry is a good man—very levelheaded."

Clair smiled. "I will tell him you said so, Mr. Holmes."

Holmes turned back to Danny. "Wiggins, I will leave you now. I think I have enough information from here. Farewell, and remember what Reverend Henry said. It will keep you out of trouble. By the way, Mr. Hanson has a decidedly German accent . . . like the murdered scientist. It remains to be seen whether that is significant or not." Holmes dashed to catch a cab that was passing the front steps of the church.

Danny spoke to Peachy. "I think we need to investigate further. Clair, can you take Duff home tonight? Peachy and I have some work to do."

Peachy looked at him questioningly.

"Trust me," Danny said.

Clair nodded, and Danny grabbed Peachy by the shirtsleeve, leading him down the street.

When they were far enough away not to be overheard, Danny spoke. "There were things I noticed today while Holmes and I were at the site. We passed side tunnels that Holmes barely glanced at. He was only interested in seeing the collapse, but I know there's more down there."

"So what?" Peachy asked. "What's that got to do with us?"

Danny spoke with the voice of a leader. "We are going to the site again. Now. Tonight."

●●●

North of Oxford Street, Tottenham Court Road was the location of many professional and educational establishments. The avenue was home to the University of London, the London School of Tropical Medicine, the Architectural Association, and the headquarters of the newly formed East Africa Company, as well as various banks and law firms.

It was also deserted. By the time Danny and Peachy explored it in the night hours after the protest meeting, all the dons, solicitors, barristers, bankers, and clerks had long since gone home.

Danny located a fenced-off area. "Must be an air shaft," he whispered to Peachy.

Climbing over the fence, he dropped down inside the barrier. When he whistled softly, Peachy joined him.

Shivering in the chill air, Peachy watched as Danny pulled a box of matches from his pocket to light a candle. Danny lay flat on his belly with his head inside a vertical shaft.

"How far down is it?" Peachy muttered.

"Just wait half a tick," Danny called. His voice echoed hollowly. "This pipe is thicker than I thought." Danny scooted farther in, until his feet were the only things Peachy could see. "It looks like it's a lot higher, too."

Peachy winced. "How much higher?"

"About seven or eight feet down to a ledge. Enough to where we'll have to use the rope when we want to come back out."

"Oh, blimey," Peachy muttered to himself. And then to Danny: "Can we make it?"

"'Course," Danny called. "Piece of cake. Come on."

Danny wriggled back out to the air and attached a length of rope to one of the fence posts. Then he dropped the coil into the shaft. "Let's go," he said, sliding down with the candle in one hand and his feet clamped on the cable.

Peachy took one last look for anyone who might be coming. It seemed he was hoping for an interruption—some reason why they should not do this. Finding none, he sighed and called, "Are you clear? I'm coming down."

"Watch out, Peach," Danny instructed. "This mud's pretty deep. Hang on a minute while I get the other candle lit."

Gripping the rope, Peachy stopped halfway down. He hung there, swaying like an abandoned puppet. Another match flared brightly in the darkness, forcing Peachy to turn away his eyes.

Danny held the light low to the ground, scouting for a drier place where Peachy could land. "I see a spot for you," he said, squatting down. "It's just left of where your feet are dangling."

Peachy peered down. Danny was standing on a ledge in a muddy puddle. The mud was deep enough that it made a sucking sound when Danny moved his feet.

Sliding farther down a little at a time, Peachy at last hung just above the bottom. Spotting the place that Danny had mentioned, he swung himself sideways, and when he let go of the rope, he landed on dry ground.

Danny sighed. "Nice jump, Peachy. I didn't know you were a gymnast."

"With the right guidance I can do anything."

Danny chuckled. "Too right! A little guidance is what we need right now. Where do we go from here?"

"It's too bad Duff isn't here. I'll bet he knows this whole place by now," Peachy replied, looking around. "There's a pair of lanterns on the wall."

They each grabbed one and lit it. The additional light revealed a sloping passageway running down into the depths of the earth.

"Here we go," Danny said, leading the way.

Peachy hesitated a few seconds before following. He usually liked adventure, but there was something about being this far under the ground that he wasn't crazy about. . . . But not wanting to be left behind in the tunnel, he hurried to catch up with Danny.

Soon the boys reached the enormous steel-paneled walls that arched upward above concrete foundations. A black-iron ladder let them down the last twenty feet to the tunnel floor.

The long, dark cavern with its ribbed supports reminded Peachy of the backbone of a fish, seen from the inside. He imagined that he was Jonah from the Bible story, trying to find a way out of the belly of the whale. But the way the lanterns made the rough edges flicker and move made the thought too creepy. A minute later he was sorry he had thought of it. Feeling a draft, he observed, "We must be getting near an opening."

"I know," Danny responded. "I'd almost forgotten how cold it was outside."

They walked a hundred more yards. Suddenly a shaft of light beamed out from the side of the tunnel. At first it seemed to be coming from a crack in the earth itself.

"Peachy, look!" Danny whispered.

The glow was coming from a small side tunnel, its entrance hidden behind a canvas-and-wood barrier. The canvas was painted gray and splashed with rock dust so it blended in with the tunnel wall. If the yellow light had not outlined its edges, the two friends would have missed finding it.

"There must be someone back there. Come on, Danny."

Danny stopped in his tracks. "I was right here today and didn't see this."

"Shhh," Peachy hushed him, blowing out his lantern. "I heard someone."

Danny did the same, and they were left in complete blackness except for the shaft of light.

A man's voice could be heard arguing in piercing cockney tones. "I don't nefer do this sorta thing, Gov. I don't even like the old rat. But when ol' Riley says sometink, 'e means it. Gi' us a drink, then."

Peachy made a face to show he did not understand.

When the man continued to talk aimlessly, and no other voice responded, Peachy realized that the man must be talking to himself. "The bloke's crazy," he hissed.

"Listen," Danny said, hushing Peachy.

"It's blinking nonsense."

"Shhh," Danny insisted. "He may give away something yet."

"Tamarrah I'll be rich. Hit's the truth," the man said in a gleeful tone. A loud clank, as of a piece of metal striking other metal, sounded, and the man's footsteps could be heard coming toward the opening.

"Let's go," Peachy whispered urgently. "He's coming."

The Baker Street Irregulars took off up the main tunnel. The light grew behind them as Peachy looked back. Finally a lantern appeared in the open, and a man set the lamp down in the middle of the tracks and lifted the sheet of wood and canvas back into place.

At that very moment, Peachy tripped over a railroad tie and tumbled to the ground with a thud.

Danny quickly flattened his body to the ground. The boys were only a few feet apart.

The man stopped his work and looked around for the source of the unexplained noise. Picking up the lantern again, the unknown man slowly crept toward them. He walked almost to the point where it seemed he would step on Peachy.

Just before stomping on Peachy's back, he stopped, with the lantern held above his head. Then he swung quickly around in the opposite direction. "Who is that?" he cried in a trembling voice.

"Relax, Riley. It's Gamble," another voice called.

"Oh, you put me up a proper dewskitch, you did," Riley complained. "Frazzled my wits! I thought hit was the ghost of Chas, comin' back to get me."

A chill ran down Peachy's back with the mention of the word *ghost*. Then the chill turned to icy spikes when Peachy remembered that Chas was the name of the man who had died in the tunnel cave-in.

A spooky whisper called out from the blackness, "Riley, I want revenge."

All grew silent as Riley got nervous again. "Gamble . . . ," he called. "Gamble, is that you?"

Peachy grew even more fearful. What if there really was a ghost?

The soft moaning voice beckoned to Riley again. "Riley, I'll take no less than your heeeaad."

"Gamble! It ain't funny no more." Gamble still did not reply, and by then Riley really started to scream. "Gamble! Chas has come back from the deeeaaaad." Riley dropped the lantern in his panic.

"Take it easy, Riley," Gamble's voice said. "You've just got the wind up. Chas is not coming back. He's dead and gone." The man named Gamble walked into Riley's lantern light.

"His ghost is 'ere," Riley pleaded. "You've gotta get me out of this place." Riley spun in circles, as if expecting to find someone who was always behind him.

"Stow it, Riley. You must be hearing things. Come on, let's go have another nice drink and calm down."

"But the work on the other tunnel," Riley argued. "I've gotta finish tonight."

"Later," Gamble said with authority as they walked off. "Right now you need to calm down."

Peachy and Danny waited until the men's light was totally gone before moving. Danny rushed over to where Peachy lay. "I can't believe you, Peachy," Danny whispered with excitement, helping his friend to stand.

Peachy reached up and took Danny by the wrist. "Believe what?"

"The way you caught on to the spook gambit."

"You mean—" Peachy paused as iciness paralyzed his spine— "you didn't do it?"

"Come on, Peachy," Danny argued. "It was you."

"Are you glocky? I was right on the ground in front of the bloke. Why would I go and take a bloomin' chance like that for?"

"It must have been Gamble."

"Righto. It must have been," Peachy replied. He hoped he could convince himself. "Sound does play funny tricks down here, you know."

"I think we've seen enough," Danny said, echoing Peachy's thoughts exactly. "There's nothing much to this after all."

"That's what I think, too," Peachy agreed. "We can go now and it won't matter. Do you think it's safe to light the lantern?"

Danny pulled the box from his pocket and had the match already lit before he could even have answered. "Good idea."

• • •

When Peachy and Danny were once more outside the tunnel, they panted for air and doubled over, out of breath. Their route back to the Waterloo Bridge and home took them past the foreman's shack at the construction site.

Through a knothole in the fence they could see that there was a light in the window. "I'll bet the plans are in there," Peachy said, pointing.

Danny considered what Peachy was suggesting. The moon was out now, casting eerie shadows over everything. He turned to

Peachy. "Should we chance it? We made it this far. Is it worth the risk of being caught after all we've been through?"

"Is it worth the price of what could happen if we leave the site without finding out something?" Peachy ticked off the clues on his fingers. "We know that the suspicious bloke I saw in the alley is connected to the foreman. We know that the acid that showed up on Duff's trousers is hooked to a murder and that Duff got it here in the tunnel. We know that even Holmes now believes something criminal is going on. What we don't know is how it ties together. If we locate those plans, maybe they will tell us."

"Right. Splendid." Danny sighed, sinking down lower and tilting his head back. He hated to admit it, but he knew Peachy was right. If they wanted to find the answer to the mystery, they had to be persistent. They had to pursue their goal.

Peachy sat up to look at Danny. "I know it's a big risk, but I'll bet it pays off to look for those plans. We may save Clair's church or uncover the mystery to those accidents. Who knows?" He stood to look through the fence again. All was quiet.

Danny proposed the consequences. "What if those blokes from the tunnel come back?"

"They're off somewhere getting liquored up, remember?" Peachy studied the window of the office. He could see a couple of desks, a drafting table, a file cabinet, and a chalkboard, but no one moving about. "Besides, there's no one in there."

Despite Danny's misgivings, the two were soon over the fence and into the compound. Danny said hopefully, "The door's probably locked anyway."

But it wasn't. Peachy peeked into the window and shook his head. "It's empty. Come on." He pushed open the door.

Danny followed Peachy closely, carefully shutting the door behind them. "Look at all these piles of papers," he said ruefully. "Where will we begin?"

"Wherever they keep the plans," Peachy replied. "That's all we care about."

Danny hurried over to the filing cabinet and opened the top

drawer. In it he found layer upon layer of files, each filled with plans.

"They've got to be classified by date—the day they were signed out or something," Peachy called, while searching one of the desks.

"The twenty-second of January is what we want," Danny said, while flipping through the folders. "These are all old. They're dated last year." He squatted down to try the bottom drawer. It was locked. "There may be more in this other drawer, but I can't get it open."

Peachy continued his search in the desk. "Nothing here but a bunch of pencils and drawing paper." Frustrated, he banged the drawer, causing the pencil case to jump. "What's this?" he said aloud as he pried it up. "Oy, Danny! I found a key hidden in the desk." He picked it up and took it to Danny. "It looks like it might fit." When he wiggled it into the tiny lock on the file drawer, the lock made a promising click, and the latch on the cabinet released.

"Wizard! Well done, Peachy!" Danny patted him on the back.

Both of the boys squatted down to search the files. There were only a few, and they quickly went through most of them. But none of the information seemed like what they were looking for.

"Here it is," Peachy exclaimed at last, pulling out a set of folded papers. "The twenty-second of January," he read off the top right-hand corner.

Now that they had located the plans in question, neither boy was sure what it meant. "What is it we're looking for?" Peachy wondered aloud. "I'll bet Holmes would know. Should we just write the numbers down and look up the plans later? Then we can get out of here."

"Hold on." Danny reached into his pocket. "I've got something better." He pulled out the piece of pink claylike goo that Sherlock Holmes had given him.

"What's that?" Peachy asked curiously.

Danny stuck the material over the plan numbers and pressed it down. "It's one of Holmes' inventions. I forgot to tell you about it." He removed the soft pink glob to show Peachy.

"It lifts the numbers right off the page!"

"Righto," Danny said.

Danny concealed the copying substance in the sleeve of his jacket. He was concerned that the numbers might wear off, so he slipped it in facing his skin. Peachy rushed the key back to the desk, replaced it under the pencil case, and closed the desk drawer once again. Then he grabbed the plan from Danny, shoved it back in the file cabinet, and locked it up as well.

"Come on. Let's get out of here," Peachy said.

Danny buttoned up his coat on the way out as Peachy closed the door, making sure that it was locked securely.

Once they were outside, Danny pointed to a massive dirt pile by the side of the fence. "Come on, Peachy. We can hide behind that while we get over the fence."

They crept over to the shelter of the rubble heap and sighed with relief. On the other side was freedom and safety.

"Give me a lift," Peachy whispered to Danny. "Then I'll pull you up."

Danny squatted down and laced his hands together. He was just about to lift Peachy's foot when a voice shouted, "Stop! Trespassers! Stop right there!" Then a shrill, two-tone police whistle sounded.

Peachy scrambled up the fence, and Danny followed, climbing as fast as he could. He was just inches from the top rail when someone yanked his foot down. Danny fell onto the hard, frozen ground. A second later, he saw Peachy land next to him, even harder.

It was three against two. Three guards against two boys. Danny and Peachy didn't have a chance.

"Vandals or saboteurs, eh?" one of the guards growled. "You're done for! It'll be Newgate Prison for both of you!"

Eight

Duff had to leave for work so early in the morning that Clair did not get up to take him. But that did not mean she had forgotten her promise. Her father's carriage appeared outside the Waterloo Road Ragged School, and Duff was transported to his job with time to spare. He wondered what had happened to Danny and Peachy, then shrugged and set to work.

Almost instantly he got into trouble with Billy. It was as if the boy had been watching for Duff's arrival in order to torment him. "Get up the tunnel," Billy snarled. "Take a shovel and your wheelbarrow. I want you loading *and* unloading today."

Duff agreed without complaint, even though the arrangement would mean twice as much work for him. Soon he found himself all alone, far down the dark shaft.

After shoveling and wheeling three loads all the way back to the dumps at the entrance, Duff discovered on his fourth trip that he had company—Billy and Riley.

"There's other parts of the work that need inspecting," Riley was urging Billy. "You should go."

"Soon," Billy countered. "I want to see that this lazy oaf isn't leaning on the shovel when no one's around."

"I'm workin'," Duff argued. He didn't like this boy's attitude . . . *at all*. Why was he being so mean? Duff hadn't done anything to him.

"Don't back talk me," Billy warned harshly. "Mr. Ruby made me . . . assistant foreman, see. So you keep your mouth shut."

Duff nodded and began to fill his fourth wheelbarrow. Best to just do his work and stay out of Billy's way.

"Young master Billy," Riley tried again, "I remember now. Your uncle wants to see you. Will you come?"

"Soon," Billy snapped with irritation. "Cut along and tell my uncle I'm busy." He stopped to stare at Riley. "What ails you, anyway?" Billy asked.

"Nothing, nothing," Riley muttered. "Ever since the explosion that killed Chas . . . you know, it was a bloomin' miracle that it didn't get to me, too. I . . . I gotta go now. You come quick as you can, eh?"

With a negligent wave of his hand, Billy dismissed Riley and turned back to harassing Duff. "Edge!" he shouted, though Duff was already digging at twice the speed of any other miner. "Quit slacking."

Five minutes passed. The air became heavy with a pungent smell, like noxious smoke. Duff, who had completed another load, started out to dump it.

"I'll be waiting for you," Billy warned. "You come straight back. Got it?"

Duff nodded. All he wanted to do was go home. Back to the Ragged School. And back to carrying newspapers for Danny and Peachy. That now seemed like the best job in the world.

A hundred yards toward daylight, Duff heard a sharp crack. The kind a tree made when it fell. But where were the trees? Confused, Duff looked around. He saw only stone, steel, and concrete.

Turning his head toward the noise, Duff saw Billy staring upward. An instant later there was another report like a rifle shot, and a concrete support pillar bulged outward and toppled toward Billy.

The curly-haired boy flung himself toward the wall of the tunnel. That action, performed by instinct alone, saved his life. Instead of being crushed by the falling rubble, it fell across him, trapping him in a pocket. "Help," he cried, "Help me!"

As much as Duff disliked Billy, he never even hesitated. Someone was in trouble—never mind that it was Billy, who had been such a bully. Duff never thought of going for help from someone else. He ran back toward the cave-in and began throwing blocks of masonry aside like a dog after a gopher.

"Are you all right?" Duff asked Billy when the top of his head appeared.

"Yes," Billy replied in a trembling voice. "Yes, I think so. But I'm still trapped."

A lump of stone dropped from overhead, striking Duff on the shoulder. Duff winced and looked up.

"Don't leave," Billy pleaded. "Don't leave me here alone."

The bullying tone had disappeared. In its place Duff heard fear.

Duff didn't tell Billy that he would never think of leaving someone who was trapped and hurt. He simply said, "I won't." After taking one second to rub his aching shoulder, he continued to dig. "I'll get you out in no time," he assured Billy.

And so he did. Within ten minutes, Billy was free. Except for a few cuts and bruises, he was uninjured. He stood with his head down. "Why'd you stay to help?" he asked Duff. "You could have been killed yourself."

"You needed help. I was closest," Duff replied.

"Yes, but why help *me?*" Billy asked. He raised his head to stare into Duff's eyes.

"Did I do wrong?" Duff asked in confusion.

"No!"

"Well then," Duff said, "I'll get back to work now." He returned to pushing the wheelbarrow, leaving behind a baffled and humbled Billy.

•••

Danny perched with his feet on the cell bars and his back to the cold, drippy wall of the holding pen of Newgate Prison. Peachy reclined uncomfortably on the stone floor beside him with his head tilted back in the corner. Both boys looked miserable to the point of tears.

The gruff jailer taunted them from a desk across the hall. "Five years for trespassing." He laughed savagely. "'Ard labor. You'll both 'ave beards before you see outside again. 'Ow do you like it so far?"

"It's no bank holiday in Brighton—that's for certain," Peachy answered quickly.

"No," the guard retorted. "'Ow'd you gutter rats like to stay 'ere for the rest o' your lives? I can arrange that, I can."

"You can't keep us," Peachy argued. "Sherlock Holmes and Inspector Avery would find out what you did, and then where would you be?"

"And 'ow'd you like it if I stick you down the 'ole with the rest o' the rats?" the sentry threatened. "Lock you up and leave you to rot, and tell ol' blinkin' 'olmes and bloomin' Avery I don't know where you went. 'Ow 'bout that?"

Peachy sobered quickly as he considered the likelihood of it happening. It could be done that way. A man could get thrown in jail for something little and die there twenty years later. After all, Peachy remembered hearing about a bloke who was locked up for fourteen years for stealing a loaf of bread. Just because the jailer didn't like him.

What had happened to all of their plans? They had taken a big risk, and it hadn't panned out. The only prayer they had now was that Holmes or Avery would somehow get wind that part of the Baker Street Brigade was locked up at Newgate.

"Peachy, you better keep mum, or we're going to be here a lot longer than we want," Danny urged his friend. "Just be patient." The boys sat quietly for a while, passing the time with thought and prayer that they would somehow get out of the mess they were in.

"I can't believe I lost the copying clay with plan numbers,"

Danny scolded himself. "I must have dropped it when they grabbed us. I'm such an idiot. The only thing we had to show for this whole disaster, and it's gone."

"It'll come right, Danny. We'll get ahold of those numbers again. Don't you worry. We'll tell Holmes about it all, soon as he gets here."

"Get up, you two," the grumpy jailer commanded.

Peachy's heart began to pound. He was more scared now than he could ever remember being. "Where are we going, sir?" he asked politely. "Home?"

"'Ome, ha!" The man laughed loudly. "You're going to the pit!"

Danny's eyes grew wide with fear, and his mouth dropped open. Peachy saw the tears in his friend's eyes and knew there were some in his own eyes, too. Could this really be happening?

"Come on! Move!" the guard yelled.

Down and down they were led, past barred security gates, then around and around a narrow spiral staircase. The passage seemed to get narrower and narrower the farther they went. The cold, the damp, and the stench reached out to grab them and pull them in. It was like sinking in ice-cold mud.

A tear rolled down Peachy's cheek as the jailer pushed him and Danny into a grimy, wet cell with bony, bearded men, who were chained to the walls. "Wait, sir, please," Peachy cried.

"You chavvies 'aven't got a prayer!" the jailer shouted, slamming the iron door with a forceful clank.

To Peachy, it felt like the closing of a coffin lid. He sank to the floor alongside Danny, and they huddled together. The only good thing about all of this was that at least the jailer hadn't chained them to the walls.

But Peachy wondered if they would ever see the light of day again.

• • •

Mr. Ruby had been overseeing the repair of the latest collapse all day and was very aggravated with the lack of progress they had made. "Now!" he yelled to the operator of a steam-powered winch.

The block and tackle was supposed to be lifting a fallen beam that had been painstakingly dug free from the rubble. The delay in executing the command to lift was just enough to allow another shower of masonry to drop over the top of the timber, binding it in the pile again.

"Where do we hire these morons?" Ruby proclaimed into the air. He turned to the worker. "Vela! How can you be so stupid?"

The man stared at the floor.

"Are you deaf? When I say 'now,' you're supposed to engage the winch. Let's get it right this time!"

As other workmen uncovered the timber again, Billy Kelly joined the group. "Afternoon," he said to the owner. "How can I help?"

"Just stand out of the way. I'll be finished in a moment. . . ."

•••

Billy did as Charles Ruby told him. He stood out of the way of the winch and watched as the harness was reconnected to the beam. Rocks and rubble were scooped away to take the weight off the top.

But then he noticed a problem. The cable had slipped under a large boulder when the tension was off. Without asking, he moved to free it.

"Now!" yelled Ruby, and Vela engaged the winch motor.

At that instant, Billy freed the cable from beneath the rock. The additional slack in the line caused the winch to overrotate, fouling the wire around the gears and knocking Billy to the ground. The winch halted suddenly, smoking and sputtering.

Billy was picking himself up when Ruby stormed over to him.

"You stupid boy! Look what you've done! You've burned up the winch. Two accidents, and you were in both!" he said, referring to Billy's earlier narrow escape.

"B-but you had it fouled under—," Billy stuttered.

Ruby backhanded him in the face. "*I* had it fouled? Are you say-ing this is *my* fault?"

"But it was under the rock . . ."

Ruby cuffed him again, and this time Billy fell down. "Don't argue with me! Now, don't you have something to do? What am I paying you for?"

Billy got up, feeling the sting of the slap on his cheek. "I was looking for my uncle," he mumbled.

"He's busy," Ruby snapped.

"Where?"

Ruby glared at Billy with hatred as he strode toward him. Grabbing Billy by the shirt collar, Ruby pulled him up on tiptoe until they were eye to eye. "I said he's busy! And you've caused enough trouble around here that if you don't clear off, I'll fire the both of you!"

When Ruby dropped Billy back to the ground, Billy scrambled away. Charles Ruby was known for his temper, but this time it was out of control, even for him.

As Billy ran the other direction, he heard Ruby's irate words to the men. "Let's get back to work! I want this space cleared, and I want it cleared tonight! Anyone who doesn't break his back to get the job done can draw his time right now!"

●●●

After rescuing Billy from the falling stone, Duff was no longer nervous about being underground. He felt God's approval, even though he could not have explained it. Somehow he knew that he was supposed to be in the tunnel if for no other reason than to have saved Billy's life.

Headmaster Ingram was always saying that everything worked out well for people who obeyed God. And even though Duff still wasn't crazy about Billy, he had obeyed. He had done the right thing and helped someone who was hurting. Maybe that was why Duff felt like God was right there in the tunnel with him now, smiling and nodding. It felt good to be a part of God's plan.

Duff also realized that he was lucky to be in the tunnel only part of the time—not because of the absence of light but because of the horrible old man who kept trying to scare him. It seemed to Duff that the ancient miner came up with a new frightening tale every time Duff would take out a load of dirt.

Like the other workmen, however, the thing that still made Duff the most nervous was a visit from one of the bosses. Most of the time the supervisors came to yell and demand faster work, just like Billy did. "Move your bloomin' backsides!" was their favorite expression, and to hear it made Duff sick.

To Duff it seemed that the supervisors played games. They took silly satisfaction in sneaking up on a group of men chatting while working and yelling, "Edge!" Duff dreaded that word, too. Just thinking of it made him work even harder. He knew he would have sore arms and legs and hands and feet again by the end of the day.

"Don't like him one bit," Duff said, giving voice to his thoughts.

"Eh, Duff?" the old man asked, but Duff did not answer.

Their group had made considerable progress on the side tunnel since Duff had begun work there, moving into the wall a good fifty feet. The lighting had not caught up with them yet, and their work was in darkness except for three candles, which rested on iron spikes. Duff waited patiently for a full wheelbarrow load so he could return to the sunshine again.

"Duff!" a voice yelled from the mouth of the side passage. It was Billy.

Duff grimaced. What would Billy be up to now?

Billy stormed into the work area and headed straight for him. "Duff!" he yelled again. "Where are you? Are you hiding?"

"No, sir," Duff replied. He could hear his voice shaking, and he did not like it.

"You've been standing about there awhile, haven't you?"

Was the question a trick to get him in trouble? "No, sir, I'm busy."

"I'm not here to yell at you," Billy said. "I need to know if you've seen my uncle."

Duff thought hard. "No. I been workin' hard. I ain't seen hardly nobody."

When Billy stepped toward him, Duff cringed, expecting to be slapped.

Instead, Billy patted him on the back. "I know you do. I know you work hard."

Confused, Duff looked at Billy for an explanation.

"I'm sorry," Billy said quietly. "I can see now that I was wrong for yelling at you. You helped me. Maybe even saved my life. You're the only person who's ever been nice to me. . . ."

Duff noticed that the other men had stopped working and were standing, shovels in hand, listening.

"Thank you," Billy said. There was a glint of a teardrop in his eye.

Duff studied Billy. What had changed him?

"Please, Duff," Billy continued, "if you see my uncle, you must—"

"Billy boy, there you are," a voice said from behind him. It was a man Duff did not recognize. He was large and muscular with a receding hairline. He wore a pair of coveralls and a white undershirt. Duff could not see his face.

"Hello, Mr. Gamble," Billy said, swiping at his eyes. "What is it?"

"Your uncle just came by the shack and told me to find you. He wants you to come here at seven tonight to help manage a late shift that starts at eight. We're way behind on cleanup, and Ruby is raising merry ned."

Billy started to leave, but Gamble caught his arm. "He's already gone. He said to meet him here at seven." Billy shook his arm loose from the man's grip and strode past him.

"Well, what are you looking at?" Gamble yelled at Duff. "Get back to work! Edge!"

Nine

Thick patches of black mold carpeted the damp, musty walls. A bearded man dressed in rags was in the corner of Danny and Peachy's cell. The decrepit prisoner wheezed and coughed, cleared his throat, and spit across the cell toward the boys. "Hey you," the scraggly man shouted, motioning. "Why don't you move out of the way? You're blocking my view."

Danny's whole body drooped. His eyes were half closed, and he was trying to pretend that he was somewhere else . . . anywhere else. He felt like he was going crazy, and it had been only a few hours.

"Oy! Are you deaf?" The ragged man spat again. This time it landed on Danny's boot.

Danny scrambled to his feet, startled. "I'm no sneak thief!" he yelled back.

"I said move out o' me way!" growled the bearded prisoner, showing the brown stumps where his teeth had been. He screamed in rage, banging and clanking his shackles on the filthy bars.

Covering his ears, Peachy also closed his eyes. "Stop!" he pleaded at the top of his lungs.

At that point the whole dungeon was aroused. All the prisoners began clanking their shackles and rattling their chains.

Peachy continued to scream. Danny huddled closer to him. Both of them were shivering like scared animals.

The bearded prisoner crouched on one foot in the corner and bounced rapidly. Leaning his head from side to side, he stared at Danny and Peachy through first one eye and then the other. Only one eye was dead, Danny noticed—lifeless and staring at everything while seeing nothing.

"You!" the prisoner said. "What are you staring at?!"

Peachy stiffened. "Nothing!" he replied. "Not you or anyone. We don't belong down here."

The man growled again, a guttural sound like a caged tiger. It was followed by a low, nonhuman humming. "*Hmmm. Hmmm. Hmmm.* They don't think they belong here! Come over here and let me see you."

"Why?" Peachy questioned. "You can see us just fine."

"My sight," the man whimpered. "It's not so good since me partner knocked me out with a gaffer's hook."

"We're fine right here," Peachy insisted bravely.

Danny felt something tug at his jacket from behind. It startled him, and he turned abruptly. A pair of men reached through the bars behind them, trying to grab Peachy and Danny both.

"Danny, look out!" Peachy warned, pulling his friend to safety in the middle of the cell.

All around the tiny cell, men from all sides began to close in on them. Hands reached for them. Arms dangled between bars. Voices called, "Come 'ere. Come 'ere. Let me look at you."

Peachy and Danny spun in circles, trying to avert the hands. The chanting grew louder and louder until the man in the corner leaped toward them, arms outstretched to grab. Danny and Peachy jumped back to escape his reach. An iron collar around his neck yanked him to the floor, but the boys were still not safe. A host of hands grasped their arms and legs, pinning them back against the bars.

"Stop!" a thunderous voice commanded. It was a jailer with a long clublike cane. He thumped and prodded at the attackers. They let go of the boys, who scurried once again to the middle of the cell.

The prisoners screamed and retreated to the farthest corners. There they huddled, swatting at the jailer's cane as if it were a deadly wasp.

"Silence!" the jailer demanded. He had the ability to make any one man's life even more miserable than it already was, so the room did become silent. "Come on, you two." He motioned to the boys. "It looks like you're to be sprung."

The boys rushed to the gate, shaking the bars until it was opened.

"Not fair! Not fair!" the whole mob of prisoners began to shriek as the boys hurried up the stairs.

Danny and Peachy could hear the chant continuing even after they reached the ground floor. The guard led them around to the booking desk. There, to their complete happiness, stood Sherlock Holmes.

"Hello, my little wharf rats." He smiled. "Did you have a nice stay at Royal Newgate Hotel?"

They rushed to him.

"Mr. Holmes, are we glad to see you!" Peachy panted. "We was almost killed in there."

"You know these chavvies?" the warden asked.

"They are part of the Baker Street Brigade. My Irregulars."

Danny and Peachy sighed in relief.

"Righto. Then suppose you give them what for about trespassing and what will happen next time. Sign here." The guard pointed to their release form.

Holmes eyed both boys. "I'm sure they'll rethink their lives after this."

Once outside, Holmes escorted them to a cab. It was late in the afternoon, and the sun was shining.

Danny wanted to just stand there for a long time and soak in the light. He'd thought he'd never see it again. How had Holmes found them?

"Danny, Peachy," Holmes said in a serious tone, "I'm quite disappointed that you would do something illegal. And, frankly, I'm annoyed that you did not consult me first. You must realize that everything I'm capable of doing, you are not. And if you break the law, you'll be punished if caught." He stopped to look at them sternly.

"But, Mr. Holmes," Danny pleaded, "we found some plans in a drawer with the same date as when Peachy saw the boy in the alley."

The consulting detective narrowed his eyes. The lecture abruptly ended. "Tell me more."

"Danny used the pink glob that you gave him to copy the file numbers," Peachy bragged, as if anxious to make amends for displeasing Holmes.

"Wonderful," the sleuth exclaimed. "Where is it?"

Peachy and Danny looked at each other and then at the ground with disappointment.

"I lost it when we were nabbed," Danny answered.

Holmes exhaled in exasperation. "Then it is of no use."

"But can't we go look up the plans, now we know that they have them?" Peachy asked.

"I'm afraid not," Holmes replied. "Not even I would be able to look through the thousands of confidential plans that may be registered."

"But we know that the plans are there," Danny protested. "Can't the bobbies go look?"

"Sadly, my friends, we can do nothing," Holmes insisted. "This affair has grown into a full-scale criminal operation of massive proportions. The law can do nothing until more evidence is given."

Danny slumped in defeat.

Holmes placed his hands on their backs. "I applaud your attempts to make good. And remember, I have not been idle. I have sent cables about our friend Hanson. We'll get a break yet." When he patted the boys on the back, Danny knew Mr. Holmes had forgiven them for their rash acts.

As the boys got into the waiting cab, Holmes added, "Now go straight home and change those filthy clothes." He chuckled. "Better still, burn them."

"Thanks for getting us out, Mr. Holmes," Peachy said gratefully.

Danny joined in. "I don't know what we would do without you."

"Anything for my friends." Holmes smiled and waved his ever-present pipe. "But next time, warn me ahead of any adventures you may plan, so that I may look for you here when you go missing."

Danny flinched at the memory of the prisoners and the hands reaching through the bars. "I don't think that will be anytime soon."

Holmes paid the driver and ordered, "Waterloo Road Ragged School, please."

The driver snapped the reins, and they were off.

Danny breathed easier once they were out of the shadow of Newgate Prison.

• • •

Billy stood outside the London Messenger Service office with his hand on the doorknob. He looked nervously around. Could someone be following him? When he saw no one in sight, he grew confident enough to step inside.

He joined the queue to wait his turn. The pale green walls made him sick to his stomach.

"May I help you?" a clerk asked the boy. In the background, a continuous tapping could be heard throughout the room as dozens of tiny keys rapped away on their telegraph pads.

Billy set a handful of change on the counter. "Yes. I need to send an urgent message."

"Special delivery or regular route?"

"Special delivery, please," Billy answered, studying the chalked prices on the board behind the counter.

The clerk grabbed a form and began to fill in the details. "It's more expensive," he informed Billy.

"Do I have enough there?" Billy asked.

"If you keep it short."

"It's very urgent! It must go out as soon as possible." Billy checked the clock on the wall, which showed a quarter after five.

"Whom is it to?"

Billy cleared his throat. "To Mr. Sherlock Holmes."

That definitely got the clerk's attention. "Sounds important," he commented and leaned closer to Billy, as if hoping he'd tell more. "And what would you like it to say?"

Billy thought a minute so he would say the right things to be convincing. "Urgent regarding Central Line tunnel. My uncle, the foreman, has disappeared. He may be in danger. I have news about accidents."

●●●

"Am I glad to be out of that place," Peachy exulted as the cab clattered along Fleet Street.

"What time is it?" Danny asked suddenly.

"How should I know?" Peachy retorted. "I've been locked up, same as you. What I know is that we should meet Duff at work. Clair saw him off this morning, but she might not know to pick him up."

"You're right," Danny said. "Duffer wouldn't know what to do if we didn't come. Besides, this case is over for us. We've lost all the leads. Now it's up to Holmes. Let's get a good meal and some better sleep tonight."

Peachy nodded and hammered on the trapdoor in the roof of the hansom cab. The driver slid back the partition and asked what was wanted. "Take us to the underground dig on Tottenham Court Road," Peachy said.

"If I do, you'll walk home," the driver insisted. "I've been paid just enough for a short trip across the river, not a tour of the town."

"It's all right," Danny announced. "We have to meet a friend."

Upon arriving at the tunnel site, Danny and Peachy encountered the protesters holding their signs outside the gates and chanting various antiunderground slogans. Those opposed to the excavation linked themselves arm in arm, so that no one could pass. A thin blue ribbon decorated each coat.

"Who needs an underground? Shake the city down!" they cheered as the boys approached.

"Cor!" Peachy exclaimed. "I forgot about these blokes. What do they think they can accomplish?" As he said this, he tried to cross their line by going under the arms of two ladies. But the picketers squeezed together, blocking him out. One of them was Hanson, the suspected terrorist. Peachy drew back in alarm, tried to cross a different place, and was rebuffed by two old ladies with umbrellas held like drawn swords.

"Blimey! What's the idea?" Peachy complained. "I'm not here to work. I'm here to pick up my friend."

As though they all had trained responses, one of the women said, "If you don't support the underground, you won't support its workers."

"I suppose that's what they can accomplish, Peachy." Danny smirked at his baffled friend. "As long as they don't burn, bomb, or throw acid, they can make their point this way."

They walked down the line together looking for Clair, hoping she would be able to let them in.

"Well, if it isn't the Baker Street Irregulars," a familiar voice said. "Come to join the protest?" It was Clair, and she was holding a handful of blue ribbons and safety pins. As she spoke, she pinned a ribbon on Peachy. "I saw what happened. This should be your pass to go get Duff."

"What about that Hanson bloke?" Peachy worried. "Is he square-rigged? Is he on the level?"

"Oh—" Clair laughed—"he was just worked up. He apologized to Reverend Henry for speaking so harshly. Said he knew he was out of line."

Danny removed his jacket to straighten out his rumpled clothes before Clair pinned a ribbon on him. "That's a relief. We have nothing else to do now. We botched this case up something fierce."

"My goodness, Danny," Clair interrupted. "You need to wash yourself better! You have all sorts of black smudging on your arm."

"I do?" he asked, looking down at his mangled sleeve, which was shoved halfway up his arm. "I do!" He showed Peachy. "The numbers, Peachy! The plan numbers! That means we're still in the game! Clair, meet us at the London Surveyors' Office with Duff when he comes out. Peachy and I have to get there before they close for the day."

"B-but—," Clair stammered in futile protest.

"We'll explain later," Danny called back as they dashed off down the street.

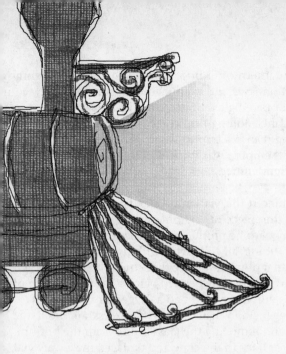

Ten

The wheels of the ore car squeaked as it rolled slowly along the track. The empty hulk moved quickly, pushed by Riley. His dark eyes squinted in the low light, and he grimaced into the darkness ahead of him. The track reached a slight rise, and he strained a little more but kept the same pace.

Riley arrived at the canvas-covered panel that disguised the hidden side tunnel. Setting the hand brake on the car, Riley groped around the inside of the bucket for his lantern, then slipped the secret door aside and entered. When he was in complete darkness, away from the main tunnel, he stopped.

Pulling a box of matches from his pocket, Riley withdrew one. In a quick motion he flicked the match head against the single front tooth he had left. The match flared in the darkness, and he lit the wick of the lantern, looking around as he did so.

On the left wall of the narrow side tunnel was a wooden crate, open at the top and filled with straw. As he got nearer, Riley saw the tops of five small, leather-covered boxes, carefully packed in the straw. Hanging the lantern on a hook behind the crate, he gently opened the clasp of one box and examined the contents.

Inside was a stoppered glass bottle, cautiously overwrapped in several layers of rubber. Riley unrolled the bottle and held it up to the light, rotating it in his grip to watch the liquid bubble and churn. The glass of the bottle was thick, and the ground-glass stopper was threaded, tightly fitted, and sealed with shiny, orange copper plating.

Riley gently replaced the vial and walked a little ways up the tunnel to fetch another piece of equipment that rested against the wall. From beneath a tarp he produced a strange contraption made of glass and copper tubing, all connected with rivets and shiny weld marks. On top it had a plunger handle that could be pushed down to pressurize a glass container suspended below. The final length of tubing looked like a gun barrel and had a trigger mounted on it.

Pulling the trigger, Riley listened to the excess air discharge before unscrewing and removing the glass bottle from the bottom. He carried the sprayer back to the crate and replaced the empty vial with the one from the box. Screwing the bottle into the place, he pumped the handle on top three times. When he gave a small pull on the trigger, a mist of the liquid was sprayed onto the wall. There it fizzed and smoked, venting a noxious smell that the man could hardly stand. But Riley watched in fascination as the few drops of liquid dissolved a hole straight through the concrete panels that had previously been melted to paper thin.

•••

The Baker Street Irregulars filed into the London Surveyors' Office, one after another, like an army of small people coming to take over. Peachy looked to see if the clerk whom he had observed with Billy was in.

Clair waved toward the deaf clerk. He walked over to the counter from his desk, carrying a piece of paper in his hand. He set it on the counter, withdrew a pen from his pocket, and began writing.

How can I help you? he wrote. The office was silent except for the scratch of his pen on the notepaper.

Clair reached for the pen and wrote, *We need to see some records. We have a number.* Then aloud, "Danny, give me the numbers."

Danny handed over a scrap of paper on which he had copied all the plan codes before he washed his arm.

Clair showed the numbers to the clerk. He nodded and smiled, then moved to some cabinets on the rear wall of the office.

When he had gone, Peachy whispered, "I don't like this. What if he's one of them?"

"Peachy," Danny scolded, "stop whispering. He's deaf. Besides, Clair said that he doesn't usually work with customers, just for that reason."

Peachy cut his protest short as the man returned with an armful of plans, all rolled up neatly and bound with small lengths of red string. Peachy and Danny took them to a corner of the counter to study. The clerk began scrawling a message again, and Clair turned to read it to the boys aloud.

One of your numbers is from the classified files. I can't show that to you. I don't even have the key.

Peachy was reading the names of the lots on the plans. "London University, Tarnan's Furs, Hopper House, Whitefield Tabernacle, Liner & Lock, Solicitors. These are all places with basements along Tottenham Court Road."

"So?" Danny questioned. "The tunnel does follow the road. He might have a genuine use for these."

Clair jotted a note back to the clerk: *Can you tell us what the classified plan is?*

Danny and Peachy were looking at a wall map of Central London, locating the buildings shown on the plans.

"Ruby got copies of all these locations along this stretch of Tottenham Court, but there's one missing," Danny said.

The clerk began writing again.

"What could that be?" Peachy asked. "Think. What's between Tarnan's and the School of Medicine? Some new business . . ."

Danny thought hard and reached the conclusion at the same time Clair shouted out the last written words from the clerk. "East Africa Company!"

Peachy had a flash of the scheme at work. Instantly he reached for the pen from the astonished clerk. *Sir,* he wrote, *we need an urgent message sent to Mr. Sherlock Holmes at 221B Baker Street. It should say, "Robbery in progress. Come to the underground dig site. We'll meet you there." Sign it, Peachy and Danny.* Turning to Danny, he demanded, "Give me some money!"

Taking a shilling from Danny, Peachy spun the paper back around to the clerk's view and handed over the coin. The clerk nodded, eyes surprised, as the Baker Street Brigade dashed from the office.

•••

When the young people had gone, the deaf clerk hurried around the room, preparing to go deliver the message. He had just put on his scarf when the alley door opened and the other clerk walked in. The deaf worker showed his superior the unusual message.

The man gasped. His hands began to tremble. He set Peachy's note down and wrote, *I will go to the messenger service and send this. You close up for the day.*

Once outside the alley door again, the superior crumpled the urgent call for Sherlock Holmes into a ball and pitched it in the trash heap. Then he hailed a cab. "Victoria Station," he ordered. "Don't spare the horses either. I'm trying to catch the channel steamer at Dover."

•••

Riley backed a small steam engine with an ore car attached northward up the track. Smoke poured from the miniature stack, obscuring the string of kerosene safety lights that lined the walls. Riley slowed the engine to a crawl, then pulled up and stopped beside the secret side tunnel.

Hopping down from the low platform of the work engine,

Riley removed the camouflaged entrance cover. "Cor blimey, Riley," he said cheerfully to himself. "After all this work, you're going to be a rich man, you are."

Riley lifted the wood-and-canvas barrier. He carried it past the front of the train and dumped it carelessly. Clapping his hands, Riley brushed them off as he returned to the ore car. Leaning over the side into the bucket, Riley retrieved the copper-and-glass spraying contraption.

Whistling happily, Riley strolled up the side tunnel with the apparatus. Stopping along the way to light other lanterns, Riley carried the sprayer into a small chamber at the far end. The room had a dirt floor and walls, but there was a concrete ceiling overhead.

"Ha," he chuckled. "One more time, darlin'," he addressed the spray rig. "Show me what you can do."

Pumping the lever on the copper mechanism, Riley pressurized the bottle. From his pocket he took a set of goggles and a breathing mask made of heavy cloth and put them on.

Holding the sprayer above his head, Riley soaked the underside of the ceiling over a chalk-marked spot about four feet long and four feet wide. A tremendously strong vapor began to fume as the liquid bubbled into the masonry. The mist carried with it an odor that was almost completely intolerable. Riley blinked at the smell, stepping back some distance away to let the acid do its work.

The ceiling began to look as if it were boiling. Slowly, bits of concrete dropped to the ground. After a couple of minutes, layers peeled away and fell to the tunnel floor. Riley watched as the highly caustic chemical burned through the solid cement.

Riley waited about half an hour for the fumes to clear before pumping the sprayer again. Getting as close to the pile of acid-eaten cement as he could without being directly under it, he painted the ceiling with another coat. This time inch-thick chunks fell. He put the sprayer aside.

Humming merrily, Riley grabbed a shovel from where it leaned against the wall. Turning its point side toward the ceiling, he scraped loose the remaining concrete. It broke off like soft mud in fist-sized lumps. When he had finished, a hole the size of the ore car had been bored through the foot-and-a-half-thick concrete, revealing the underside of the gray marble tiles of a floor above.

Riley took a long, steel pipe and began to knock upward on the tile. It cracked with a sudden snap and broke into five large pieces. Riley jumped back as the stone hunks tumbled down with a crash.

"Ha!" he yelled, delighted with his success. "Let's see what we've got here."

Holding up a lantern, Riley climbed a ladder into the newly opened crevice. Inside the space above, Riley could see glistening shelves within an eight-foot-square windowless room. On every shelf, from floor to ceiling, were stacks, heaps, and bundles of gleaming gold ingots.

"Oh yes, mate!" Riley exulted. "I'm richer than the bloomin' queen!"

●●●

Billy sat against a pile of planks as he waited for Sherlock Holmes to arrive. He scuffed his black-booted feet in the dusty earth, turning them an orangish brown. He was nervous.

Pulling on his pocket-watch chain, he opened the silver-plated timepiece and read the numbers. *Quarter to seven*, he said to himself. *Where is he?*

He had summoned Holmes two hours ago, yet the sleuth had not come. Perhaps he did not get the telegram. The idea sent shivers down Billy's spine. He knew that something was amiss, that his uncle would be in need of assistance, if he was not . . . already dead.

Rising from his seat, Billy paced in a circle. *I'll wait till 6:55*, he thought. *Then I must go in alone.*

●●●

Riley heaved gold bar after gold bar onto a long board that acted as a chute. Bent over and sweating, he threw another one. It landed on the board, slid through the opening, and landed on the heap in the tunnel with a soft thud. Riley enjoyed how the pure gold did not clank or clink like other metal. It made a solid, satisfyingly heavy sound.

The thief finished unloading an entire shelf of bullion, which took him almost twenty minutes. He looked around the enormous vault and counted ten other shelves. Each shelf had a stack five bars high and forty bars long. Each bar weighed exactly 120 ounces and was valued at four hundred British pounds. One bar alone was worth enough to provide a comfortable living for a family for a year. The total was staggering: one million British pounds. The newspapers had gotten it exactly correct. The newly formed East Africa Company, with offices on Tottenham Court Road, was capitalized to buy coffee plantations on Mount Kenya for a cool million. The gold had been due to be shipped out by heavily guarded train and fast steamship in only two days' time.

But not now.

Riley's share of the take was one-third. Enough to keep him in style for the rest of his life, if he lived like a king. Overjoyed, he figured that even if he lived to be a hundred years old, it would still take him a hundred more to spend it all.

"Riley," Gamble called. "This gold is piling up down here. Get down and help me move it into the handcart."

"Righto," Riley replied, tossing another bar down the slide. He turned to the gold stacks, blew a kiss, and said, "I'll be back, darlin's." Then he scooted down the chute, landing feetfirst on the pile of ingots. He looked up from the glitter, and his eyes met those of Charles Ruby. "We're rich, boss!" Riley exclaimed.

"I know," Ruby answered sternly. "Now get a move on. It's taken you this long to do two shelves. Riley, there are twelve tons of gold here, and we have to move it into the other tunnel. You and Gamble . . . edge! I'll go get our slave labor."

Riley turned back around happily. "Oh, how I love to play with my gold."

Ruby uncoupled the ore car from the engine, then released the brake. The tiny locomotive forced out a cloud of black smoke and chugged off down the track.

•••

Down the main shaft a short distance, Charles Ruby returned the throttle to idle and reset the brake. Then he hurried up another side tunnel. All the way to the back he hustled, seeing there in the lantern light a man shackled to an enormous ladder. It was Iron Kelly. Handcuffed, blindfolded, and gagged, the ex-foreman struggled with his bindings as Ruby approached.

"I've got a job for you, Kelly," Ruby informed him.

Kelly muttered from behind his muzzle.

"I didn't quite make that out." Ruby sneered. He pulled a pistol from his belt and poked Kelly in the lower back with it. "Now, you muck-snipe! Don't make a sudden move, or I'll blow your guts out your front!"

Ruby yanked the gag loose, then undid the handcuffs. Last he ripped off the blindfold. Kelly blinked and squinted in the sudden glare of the lantern light.

"Move, Kelly," Ruby told him, grinding the gun into his back.

"I can't see," Kelly complained. "I haven't had that thing off for two days. And I'm starving!"

"That's what you get for sneaking around my desk. Traitor! Was it for yourself, or did you turn nose on me?" When Kelly protested and tried to turn around, Ruby smacked him on the head with the butt of the gun. It practically knocked Kelly down. "Stop your whining and move."

The pair moved slowly down the path, back to the ore car. Ruby ordered his former foreman to walk up the tunnel ahead of the train. "If you try to run away, Kelly, I'll kill you. Just see if I don't!"

A minute later they were back at the other tunnel. Riley and Gamble were hard at work. "Good work," Ruby said. "Kelly here should make it easier yet. Go on, Kelly, help the men load our gold."

As Riley returned to sliding gold bars down the ramp, Kelly was forced to push a wheelbarrow down the wooden-plank walkway to the ore car. Once there he and Gamble unloaded the bullion. Ruby stood guard.

Looking up from the heap of wealth, Gamble spotted a silhouetted figure coming up the track. "Boss, look," he warned. "I think it's the kid."

"Remember to keep quiet," Ruby reminded Kelly. "You'd better smile, and you'd better act like you're going along with it."

The engine let out a burst of steam. . . .

●●●

At last Billy had found his uncle. And Ruby, Gamble, and Riley, too.

"What is all this?" he asked. "And where have you been?"

"Working nights," Kelly answered quietly.

"Cheerio, Billy," Ruby said. "Glad you're here. I want to talk to you. I'd like to make you a full partner of this operation."

"Which operation is that, sir?" Billy asked.

"Why don't you come around to the back of the car and have a look?"

Billy did as Ruby asked and staggered back at the sight. "Where . . . how . . . what is all this?" he finally blurted out.

At that instant, Riley came out of the side tunnel and ringed Billy in.

"It's gold, Billy," Ruby purred. "Your gold and my gold. Gamble's gold and Riley's gold and Kelly's, if he wants it. All you have to do is help us load it up, and you'll be rich . . . so rich you'll never have to work again as long as you live."

Billy looked to his uncle for confirmation. "Is this the ream layout? Are you in on it?"

"Run, Billy! Get away while you—," Kelly began.

Ruby bashed Kelly on the skull. The foreman fell across the ore car, his face resting on the gold bars.

Shocked, Billy took a step toward his uncle. Was he dead or simply passed out?

"Your uncle is a fool, Billy," Ruby said, leaning against the engine. "Don't throw it all away. It's a lot to throw away."

There was something very serious about Ruby's voice. *Deadly serious,* Billy thought. If he didn't play this one right, both he and his uncle might end up dead.

"What do I have to do, then?" Billy asked casually. "Kill my uncle?" *As if I could.*

"You guessed it," Ruby answered with the gun still in his hand. "Shoot him, and a part of all this is yours."

"Yes, sir," Billy answered. "I can do it." But he was really thinking, *What can I do to get us both out of this?*

"That's my boy, Billy," Ruby cheered. "Gamble, give him your gun."

Pulling a six-shot revolver from his pocket, Gamble passed it over. "Here you go, mate. Let's see if you're up to it."

Billy took the gun in his hand. It felt heavy—deadly. He turned to Ruby and looked him straight in the eye. "Isn't there any more gold to be carried out?"

"Sure there is," Ruby answered impatiently. "But what are you waiting for?"

"Why don't we use him to help carry before we get rid of him?"

Ruby laughed. "Brilliant, Billy. You think just like me. I appreciate a man who'd rather have someone else break their back. Give the gun back to Gamble."

When Billy handed the gun over, he realized he may have just given up his only hope to freedom and life.

•••

Watching from a distance were the Baker Street Irregulars. Danny, Peachy, and Duff were shielded from view by the gigantic corrugated-steel supports that ribbed the walls like giant horseshoes standing on the edge.

"Danny, they've got guns," Peachy whispered. "What are we going to do?"

"Shhh." Danny hushed him in a low whisper. "I was scared for a minute. Now I think Billy is stalling them. We'll just have to wait until they finish and head up to the other end again before we can move up any farther."

Minutes after Danny said that, the operation was finished. The boys heard Gamble tell Ruby that the next wheelbarrow load was the last.

"All right," Ruby agreed. "Then it's time to move out. I'll take Riley with me to start unloading. Meanwhile, you set the charges to blow the tunnel."

"You're going to blow the tunnel?" Billy exclaimed.

"That's right," Ruby agreed, nodding to Riley, who was behind Billy. "Now," he said.

Now what? Danny wondered. He peered out from behind the steel support.

All of a sudden Riley grabbed Billy and threw him to the ground. As Gamble retied Kelly, Riley bound Billy's hands behind his back. Then Riley jerked him to his feet again.

"What's this? I thought I was a partner!" Billy sputtered.

Smirking, Ruby explained, "The plans showing the connection between the vault and this spot are now in your uncle's desk. When they find your remains and a few scattered bars of gold, they'll think you two planned the crime but got caught in your own explosion. See how neatly it works out?"

"No!" Billy screamed, charging Ruby. The construction company owner tried to fire off a round, but Billy was right on him. Ruby tried to evade Billy's attack, but the youth was too fast. The boy plowed into Ruby's stomach with his head. Ruby's back hit a steel support rib, knocking all the air from his lungs. Billy began to kick violently, keeping Ruby off balance and defending himself.

Riley tried several times to take aim but kept wavering, as if afraid he would hit the boss. Finally Riley rushed in and pistol-whipped Billy from behind. The crack of the revolver butt on Billy's skull echoed down the tunnel.

Rubbing his stomach, Ruby picked up his pistol from the ground. "Tie him up good," he told Gamble. "I don't want him getting away and spoiling the show at the last minute. Come on, Riley.

Let's go unload. I'll send Riley back for you," he reminded Gamble. "Get busy on those charges. Oh, and Riley, go get us another couple of lanterns."

•••

"What's he doing now?" Peachy hissed. "Why'd he get down along-side the engine?"

The Baker Street Irregulars had watched the fight and heard the plan. They were ready to free Billy and his uncle as soon as it was clear. What they did not understand was what Ruby was doing all alone there beside the tracks.

"I've got it!" Danny said. "See the bundle he's burying in the gravel? Ruby is rigging a dynamite charge to explode when the engine comes back. He's planning to kill all of them and keep the gold for himself!"

"I'll bet you're right," Peachy agreed. "We've got to do something fast. Otherwise that Billy bloke and his uncle are going to die."

As the Baker Street Irregulars watched and prayed, Ruby and Riley chugged away down the tunnel in the ore train. Gamble glanced once more at the still-unconscious Kelly and his nephew and then reentered the side shaft.

"Let's go!" Danny hissed.

The three friends sprinted toward the place where the two were tied up. "Hurry," Peachy urged unnecessarily. "Move!"

Iron Kelly was groaning and starting to wake up.

"Mr. Kelly," Danny said, "wake up! You are in great danger!"

"Who are you?" Kelly mumbled.

"No time for that now! Get up! We've got to get out of here!" Danny ordered.

They had to act quickly. Any moment Gamble could return . . . or the engine could return and set off the dynamite!

Duff tried to rouse Billy. "Come on, Billy. No time for sleeping now. Get up." But the curly-haired boy could not be roused. "I can't wake him," Duff complained to Peachy. "It doesn't matter though. Here, Peachy, help me get him on my back."

Duff stooped down beside Billy, and Peachy bent to help. Together they slung Billy across Duff's shoulders in a fireman's carry.

When Peachy was helping lift Billy, he noticed the lantern light gleaming on something in the dirt. It was a set of keys. *They must have fallen from someone's pocket during the struggle,* he thought. He stuffed them into his own trouser pocket. "Ready?" he questioned Danny and Duff.

"Which way?" Kelly said, still groggy.

"The engine will come back from up that way," Danny said. "So we'll go the other."

Even carrying Billy, Duff's long legs put him in the lead, followed by his friends. Iron Kelly stumbled and staggered but hurried along as best he could behind.

Epilogue

Sherlock Holmes removed his top hat as he entered the churchyard, followed by Inspector Avery of Scotland Yard and the Baker Street Irregulars. He pointed at Danny with his cane. "Spread out!" he cried. "Find the tomb before it's too late!"

Danny followed the ivy-covered fence that bordered the left side of the graveyard. Peachy and Duff took the opposite side, while Holmes and the inspector each scouted along an aisle of headstones in the center. All were looking for the Ruby family crypt.

"Too late for what?" Avery called. "Don't keep us in suspense, Mr. Holmes. Hasn't the scoundrel already gotten away? Explain yourself!"

"Please, Inspector!" Holmes scolded. "Haven't you a mind to think on your own? All the so-called accidents were to cover the digging of the secret tunnels and to delay completion until the exact date the gold was in the vault. The second secret tunnel must come up here in the churchyard. Ruby had planned all along to kill the other witnesses, then make his escape this way. He believed that no one would be able to separate the mangled bits and pieces after the terrific explosion. If it were not for my Irregulars, there would have been two more deaths with which to charge Ruby, and no one would realize that he had not died, too."

"But how do you know he isn't already out?"

"There has not been time. He had to get out of the path of the explosion. Then he had to move twelve tons of gold by himself. He cannot have accomplished it yet. Besides, don't you see the freight wagon in the alley back there? No, Inspector. He is still in a trap of his own making."

"Here!" Danny called to the rest of the group.

"Now we shall see," Holmes said.

They dashed down the path to the place where Danny had stopped. It was an elegant stone crypt, rising four feet above the ground, carved of Italian marble. On one side were three steps down to a large, rusty, solid-iron door with a single keyhole lock in the center that went all the way through. On one long side facing the church were the names of Ruby's parents and the dates they had lived. Below that was a memorial inscription.

Holmes nodded, and Avery drew a revolver. Stepping to the iron gate, Holmes grasped it and pulled. It was stuck fast. The lock, which looked recently oiled, was still firmly fastened.

"I can't understand it," Avery said, "unless he heard us coming and is hiding below."

"Ruby," Sherlock Holmes called loudly, "we know all about your scheme. We know the second tunnel was the key to your escape. The way back is blocked. Give up, man. You are trapped."

"Key," Peachy murmured. "Key! Mr. Holmes!"

"Yes, Carnehan. What is it?"

"I found these in the tunnel after Ruby fought with Billy," Peachy reported, handing over the set of keys.

Studying them intently, Holmes remarked, "Well, well, this changes things."

"You mean he has escaped after all?" Avery cried.

"No," Danny said, "I know what he means."

Selecting a long, slender key, Holmes slid it into the lock and twisted. The lock turned slowly, squeaking and groaning, but finally it clicked.

Avery pulled on the door, but it would not budge. "I don't think it's been opened in quite—"

"Exactly!" Holmes elbowed his way past Avery, forcing him out of the way. Holmes leaned back and rammed his shoulder into the door, budging it a little. With his second blow it was clear to all that something was blocking it from the inside.

"Give Duffer a go at it," Peachy said. "He can move anything."

Duff barreled into the door. It slid open three more inches and vented a thick cloud of noxious fumes. With one more heave the door was open.

Duff scrambled backward at the sight, falling against the steps. He turned and ran to Danny.

The others peered curiously inside. Stacked there was an enormous amount of pure gold ingots, gleaming in the lantern light.

And sprawled across the heap was the body of Charles Ruby. His fingernails were broken off short and bloody, his face contorted and blue.

"It appears he suffocated from the smoke of the explosion when he got here and discovered he could not open the crypt. He knew from Riley's earlier escape from a detonation that he would be safe from the force of the blast, but he had not reckoned on what the fumes from the acid would be like," Holmes said. He shook his head. "Killed by his own greed. An early entombment in his family's grave."

Fitting end, Danny thought. But still he shivered. The best-laid plans weren't worth much in the end if they were for evil. They would never succeed.

Headmaster Ingram was right. Wanting something a lot and going after it weren't enough. They were nothing, in fact, without knowing if you were on the right track first. And that only came from praying about it first. Making sure your heart was right, and you were going after the right thing.

As Danny stood there pondering Ruby's end and his own heart, Holmes lit his pipe.

"Come, gentlemen," the detective said. "Our work here is done. The police will take charge of the body and the gold. Our concern is with the living. Let us go see how Billy and his uncle are recovering."

Words to Know

B

blimey—an expression of surprise

bloke—a man

C

chap—a man

chavvy—street brat

cheerio—a friendly greeting

cor—an expression of surprise

D

dewskitch—a beating, a good thrashing

dodgy—suspicious

E

edge—hurry

G

glocky—crazy or unreliable

H

hansom cab—two-wheeled carriage pulled by one horse

hawk—to sell, especially on the street

K

knackered—tired

M

mate—friend or pal

muck-snipe—homeless beggar

N

nose—an informant

O

oy—a word to get attention, like "Hey!"

Q

queue—a line of people

R

raising merry ned—causing a ruckus

raven—a lookout

ream—right, proper, genuine

righto—expression of agreement

S

shindy—a fight

square-rigged—proper, correct

T

too right—an expression of agreement

W

wizard—wonderful, marvelous

Did You Know . . . ?

The City and South London Underground Railway was eventually completed, forming the basis of the Northern Line, which still runs beneath the heart of London to this day. The building of the tunnel was plagued by unexplained accidents and strange mishaps that greatly prolonged its construction. It was not placed in service until 1890.

In 1898 the George Whitefield Tabernacle on Tottenham Court Road collapsed. The ground beneath it sank, due in part to an unused and forgotten passageway. The structure was rebuilt, damaged by bombs in World War II, and rebuilt again to become The American Church.

Want more?

Go to thoenebooks.com and click on The Baker Street Detectives for fascinating info, questions to stir your heart, mind, and imagination, and much, much more.

About the Authors

Brothers Jake and Luke Thoene have long loved Sherlock Holmes, mysteries, and the city of London—all important elements for the Baker Street Detectives series. Both attended university in London, training in film and audio productions. They have collaborated on nine novels in three different series, among them: *Mystery Lights of Navajo Mesa* and *Legend of the Desert Bigfoot* in the Last Chance Detectives series and *The Mystery of the Yellow Hands*, *The Giant Rat of Sumatra*, *The Jeweled Peacock of Persia*, and *The Thundering Underground* in the Baker Street Detectives series. They also wrote the screenplay for *The Last Chance Detectives* (Tyndale and Focus on the Family) when Jake was twenty years old and Luke only seventeen.

Jake Thoene has climbed onto the CBA best-sellers list with the titles of his timely Chapter 16 series: *Shaiton's Fire*, *Firefly Blue*, and *Fuel the Fire*. His research on domestic counterterrorism included hand-to-hand and small-arms training. His books are gutsy and realistic, foretelling the many challenges and threats that face America.

Jake teaches and researches on the West Coast, where he, his wife, Wendi, and their three sons live.

Luke Thoene has also continued the Thoene family legacy of writing. In the exciting Legends of Valor series—*Sons of Valor*, *Brothers of Valor*, and *Fathers of Valor*—Luke traces the upheavals and events of the nineteenth century through the experiences of the Sutton family and their descendants. He also produces the Thoene family audiobooks. Luke lives on California's central coast.

For more information about Jake, Luke, and other Thoene family titles:

jakethoene.com
thoenebooks.com
familyaudiolibrary.com

suspense with a mission

TITLES BY
Jake Thoene
"The Christian Tom Clancy"
Dale Hurd, *CBN Newswatch*

Shaiton's Fire

In this first book in the techno-thriller series by Jake Thoene, the bombing of a subway train is only the beginning of a master plan that Steve Alstead and Chapter 16 have to stop . . . before it's too late.

Firefly Blue

In this action-packed sequel to Shaiton's Fire, Chapter 16 is called in when barrels of cyanide are stolen during a truckjacking. Experience heart-stopping action as you read this gripping story that could have been ripped from today's headlines.

Fuel the Fire

In this third book in the series, Special Agent Steve Alstead and Chapter 16, the FBI's counterterrorism unit, must stop the scheme of an al Qaeda splinter cell . . . while America's future hangs in the balance.

for more information on other great Tyndale fiction,
visit www.tyndalefiction.com

THOENE FAMILY CLASSICS™

✪ ✪ ✪

THOENE FAMILY CLASSIC HISTORICALS
by Bodie and Brock Thoene
Gold Medallion Winners*

THE ZION COVENANT
Vienna Prelude*
Prague Counterpoint
Munich Signature
Jerusalem Interlude
Danzig Passage
Warsaw Requiem*
London Refrain
Paris Encore
Dunkirk Crescendo

THE ZION CHRONICLES
The Gates of Zion*
A Daughter of Zion
The Return to Zion
A Light in Zion
The Key to Zion*

THE SHILOH LEGACY
In My Father's House*
A Thousand Shall Fall
Say to This Mountain

SHILOH AUTUMN

THE GALWAY CHRONICLES
Only the River Runs Free*
Of Men and of Angels
Ashes of Remembrance*
All Rivers to the Sea

THE ZION LEGACY
Jerusalem Vigil
Thunder from Jerusalem
Jerusalem's Heart
Jerusalem Scrolls
Stones of Jerusalem
Jerusalem's Hope

A.D. CHRONICLES
First Light
Second Touch
Third Watch
Fourth Dawn
Fifth Seal
and more to come!

THOENE FAMILY CLASSICS™

✪ ✪ ✪

THOENE FAMILY CLASSIC AMERICAN LEGENDS

LEGENDS OF THE WEST
by Bodie and Brock Thoene

The Man from Shadow Ridge
Riders of the Silver Rim
Gold Rush Prodigal
Sequoia Scout
Cannons of the Comstock
Year of the Grizzly
Shooting Star
Legend of Storey County
Hope Valley War
Delta Passage
Hangtown Lawman
Cumberland Crossing

LEGENDS OF VALOR
by Luke Thoene

Sons of Valor
Brothers of Valor
Fathers of Valor

✪ ✪ ✪

THOENE CLASSIC NONFICTION
by Bodie and Brock Thoene

Writer-to-Writer

THOENE FAMILY CLASSIC SUSPENSE
by Jake Thoene

CHAPTER 16 SERIES
Shaiton's Fire
Firefly Blue
Fuel the Fire

✪ ✪ ✪

THOENE FAMILY CLASSICS FOR KIDS
by Jake and Luke Thoene

BAKER STREET DETECTIVES
The Mystery of the Yellow Hands
The Giant Rat of Sumatra
The Jeweled Peacock of Persia
The Thundering Underground

LAST CHANCE DETECTIVES
Mystery Lights of Navajo Mesa
Legend of the Desert Bigfoot

✪ ✪ ✪

THOENE FAMILY CLASSIC AUDIOBOOKS
Available from
www.thoenebooks.com or
www.familyaudiolibrary.com